# Confusion and Catastrophe

Margaret Ryan

Hodder
Children's
Books

a division of Hodder Headline Limited

*To Lindsay,*
*with love and thanks for all her help.*

Text copyright © 2004 Margaret Ryan
Illustrations copyright © 2004 Nicola Slater
First published in 2004 under the title *Operation Wedding*
by Hodder Children's Books

This edition published in 2006

2

A Catalogue record for this book is available
from the British Library

ISBN-10: 0 340 91792 X
ISBN-13: 9780340917923

Typeset in ITC NewBaskerville by Avon DataSet Ltd,
Bidford-on-Avon, Warwickshire

Printed and bound in Great Britain by
Clays Ltd, St Ives plc

The paper and board used in this paperback by
Hodder Children's Books are natural recyclable products
made from wood grown in sustainable forests.
The manufacturing processes conform to the
environmental regulations of the country of origin.

Hodder Children's Books
a division of Hachette Children's Books
338 Euston Road
London NW1 3BH

It was the start of another ordinary term at Cosgrove High. After the Christmas holidays everyone came back to school quite cheerful. They wore new trainers, new rucksacks or new earrings. 'Discreet earrings' as Mrs Jackson, my English teacher, calls them. School rules don't allow any that are too long or too jangly, and certainly not any that light up and play a tune. Apparently they might distract us from our work. No, really? Marc Thomas, in my class, wore flashing Rudolph socks before Christmas, but the giggling from everyone round about got them banned.

I don't have any flashing socks or my ears pierced. I have a dental brace and that's probably enough metal around my head for the moment. Not that I don't fancy having my ears pierced. I'm just not convinced that somebody sticking bits of metal through my ear lobes won't be painful.

'You won't feel a thing,' said Velvet, my best friend, who had hers done as a baby.

My boyfriend, Andy, says the same. 'There's nothing to it.'

He has a little gold stud in his left ear. It's kind of cute. But then, so is he!

But I'm still not convinced.

Mrs Polanski, an elderly friend who lives down the road, always wears long dangly earrings, but when she takes them out they leave big holes in her ears you can see daylight through. And, what happens when you lie down in the bath? Does water bubble up through the holes like a miniature jacuzzi?

'Oh, you and your imagination,' said Velvet, when I asked her about this. 'Stop thinking about it, and just get it done.'

But I'm still not sure.

Belinda Fishcake Fisher has her ears pierced. And her belly button. But she'd have a bolt through her neck if she thought it was fashionable. So would the Beelines, Belinda's gang. I call them the Beelines because they always make a beeline for Belinda. They follow her around and copy everything she does. Idiots.

We're all in the same English class, apart from Andy, who's in the year above. Mrs Jackson takes us for English in Stalag 3, our Arctic hut in the playground, and first day back, she was giving us her, 'How nice it is to see you all again' speech.

Quickly followed by the, 'And I'm sure you're all going to work really hard because this is an important term' speech.

Honestly, teachers are so predictable. So are lawyers. I should know, my mum's one, and she's totally predictable. She has three main speeches: the 'work hard at school' speech, the 'tidy your bedroom' speech, and the 'behave yourself' speech. The 'behave yourself' speech has several subsections which include: not taking any illegal substances, not getting pregnant, and not breaking the law. Mum's hoping to be made a partner in her law firm very soon, so I suppose having an underage, pregnant, dopehead daughter wouldn't be a huge advantage.

We live at 3 Pelham Way with my Grandma Aphrodite and her second husband, Handsome Harris. Mum and I hadn't met Handsome till recently. He turned up unexpectedly on Christmas Eve. All the way from Oz. All the way from the Australian mafia who are currently chasing him for some money they say he owes. He doesn't. But that's the thing about crooks. They're crooked.

We have a dog called Benson, who used to belong to our neighbour, Mrs Polanski, and a mynah bird called Mortimer. Benson's more laid-back than a week of Sundays and Mortimer swears all the time. He just loves to use rude words. I would tell you what they are, but I'm not allowed to write them down, so you'll just have to use your imagination.

I love to use 'big' words, too. I collect them, like the top of my wardrobe collects dust. I know it's odd. Many people have told me so, at great length, but I don't care.

I also don't care that our little house is a bit crowded now with mum and me, Grandma and Handsome, Benson and Mortimer living there. To say nothing of Grandma's Pets' Problems business out in the garden shed, and the assortment of animals we frequently have recuperating – one of my latest 'big' words, i.e. getting better – in the garden. But it bothers Mum. The house used to be really quiet when there was only the two of us in it. There's never been a dad living with us. He went off when he discovered Mum was pregnant with me. Couldn't cope with the responsibility apparently. Mum divorced him and hasn't seen him since.

So, for years, there was only the two of us. Then Grandma and Handsome sold the sheep farm in Oz to pay off Handsome's debts – he's not very good with money – and Grandma came to stay with us. She got us Benson and Mortimer, then Handsome turned up. He's not really handsome. Quite the reverse, I suppose. But the name suits him. His face has a well-worn look, like your favourite pyjamas or your comfy slippers. He's big and noisy and when he laughs his shoulders shake and the windows rattle. He takes up most of the sofa when he sits down and when he stands up his head hits the light shade.

He tells the most amazing stories about life in the outback. About spiders as big as plates and snakes that can slide up your shorts and bite your bum, if you're not careful. Mum sits there listening, getting paler and paler. But it's when he gets on to the crocodile wrestling and shows us the scars on his legs that Mum has to leave the room. Even though she knows Handsome won the wrestling match with the croc and made a pair of boots for Grandma out of the skin, she still gets upset.

She gets upset too about so many of us living at 3 Pelham Way now. The lack of privacy makes her tetchy. And when Mum's tetchy, full body armour should be worn.

The latest tetchiness/fireworks/small volcanic eruption came about because of a piece of steak. It was just an ordinary piece of steak. It wasn't still mooing or pooing on the floor. It was just lying there on the kitchen table, annoying Mum. She's vegetarian, you see. I'm not, though I am most of the time because I eat what Mum cooks. Grandma's not, but eats what Mum cooks too because she can eat anything. But Handsome Harris isn't. Definitely isn't. He likes good red meat and plenty of it. So Grandma cooks it for him. Mum knows this, but doesn't want to see it lying around in her kitchen. But Grandma says Handsome would go belly up without it so . . .

'So, what can we do about it?' I asked Andy and Velvet at lunchtime on that first day back at school. 'Will Grandma have to cook outside on the barbie just to keep the peace? Will Handsome have to have his meals in the Pets' Problems shed just to avoid any trouble?'

'That would be a bit drastic,' said Velvet. 'Seems a shame to have Handsome eat with the sick animals Grandma's trying to cure.'

'He wouldn't mind,' I said. 'But it's not very friendly, and I like having him around. He's fun.'

Velvet bit thoughtfully into her vegetable samosa.

'Why not draw up a timetable for meals,' she said. 'Meat eaters to be finished and cleared away before veggies sit down. Or the other way around.'

'A timetable,' I said. 'Like we have in school?'

'Yes,' said Velvet. 'That's what we do in our house when we have lots of relatives come over from India to stay. We have a timetable for who gets into the bathroom first, so that people don't get cross if they're being kept late for work.'

'It's a sensible idea,' said Andy.

I nodded. 'We could certainly give it a try. Mum likes sensible ideas. She's always on at me to be more sensible.'

'She hasn't a hope,' grinned Andy and Velvet.

# 2

Mum's getting really annoyed about not being made a partner in her law firm. So much so that she updated her CV the other day.

'Perhaps I'll look for a job elsewhere,' she muttered.

I had a look at her CV. It was very impressive. She had passed all sorts of exams and had degrees in international law.

I wondered what my CV would look like.

'Perhaps I should write one out just to see,' I said to Mum.

'Why? Are you looking for a job too?' she laughed. 'The only thing you could do at the moment would be a paper round, and I don't think you need a CV for that.'

'Just the ability to get up early,' I grinned. 'Not one of my strong points.'

But I wrote out my CV anyway. Just out of interest. Did you know that CV stands for curriculum vitae which is Latin for 'the course of your life'? No, I didn't know either. Anyway, my CV.

*Name*: Abigail Montgomery.
*Age*: Thirteen years, one month, two days thirty-four and a half minutes and counting . . .
*Occupation*: Schoolgirl. No, student. That sounds more grown-up.
*Qualifications*: Cycling proficiency certificate. Fifty metres swimming certificate. Brownie badges in Baking (fairy cakes), Cooking (beans on toast), and Drawing.
*Exams passed*: English, History, French, Computer Studies.
*Exams nearly passed*: Home Economics (would have passed if I hadn't dropped the apple tart), Science (no longer allowed anywhere near a Bunsen burner since the little fire in the science lab), Art (Mad Max was very understanding about the three-legged dog in my painting when I told him it had been run over by a car).
*Exams failed miserably*: Maths (I can only cope with triangles I can TING! I'm ace at playing 'Three Blind Mice').
*Interests*: Collecting new words. My boyfriend, Andy Gray. Animals. Including helping Grandma care for the animals in her Pets' Problems business. Dog walking with Benson and Grandma and all the other dogs she walks. Aliens. (I'm sure they're out there; or may already be here.

Some teachers are definitely from another planet.)

*Other comments*: This girl has an excellent imagination and could go far.

But not far enough at times for Mrs Jackson, who says my imagination is over-fertile and will get me into trouble. Like it did the other day when I looked out of the window during English and saw aliens in the playground. How was I supposed to know the drama club were en route to the hall in the main building where they were staging a dress rehearsal for *A Midsummer Night's Dream*? There should be a law against wearing silly heads and daft costumes on a foggy January afternoon!

I just saw these strange creatures looming out of the mist and panicked. I yelled, 'The aliens have landed!' and ran and set off the fire alarm to alert the rest of the school. The school emptied in record time. Everyone in Cosgrove High lined up in the playground, and four fire engines and a police car arrived. There was no sign of any aliens. I had to go and explain to Mr Doig, the head teacher, that it hadn't really been a prank. That I really did think the aliens had landed. To be fair, Mrs Jackson stood up for me and told Mr Doig about my imagination. But he still wasn't pleased. He'd been in a meeting with the Chairman of the Board of Governors at the time.

Oops!

The rest of the school were pleased though. They enjoyed getting some time out of class and thought it was a great joke. Correction. They thought *I* was a great joke. I'll never live it down. Belinda and the Beelines chant 'Seen any aliens recently?' every time they pass me. Everyone in school now knows me as the 'Alien girl' – as if having braces, zits and corkscrew hair wasn't bad enough.

But Velvet and Andy thought it was really funny, and Grandma and Handsome said they just wished they'd been there. Mum said, 'Oh Abby, you didn't!' and put on her long-suffering expression. I don't think she'll mention it in her CV and I'm not putting it in mine!

# 3

Velvet and I are working on a timetable to make life easier at home. I tried to do it on my own, but Velvet took one look at it and shook her head.

'That'll never work,' she said.

'Why not?' I asked, slightly miffed. I'd spent ages making it. I'd even decorated it with a fancy border.

'Because,' Velvet pointed out, 'you've got Grandma Aphrodite feeding the animals in the garden at the same time she's supposed to be in the shower.'

'She could throw the food out of the bathroom window,' I suggested.

Velvet gave me her 'Now you're being an idiot' look.

'I'll help you make up a proper timetable,' she said.

'OK,' I grinned. Velvet's really sensible and organized. I think she must have been born with sensible jeans. Sorry – genes.

I wonder if that's what people who want designer babies would ask for.

'I want a baby who will sleep all night, eat boiled cabbage and have sensible genes.'

I'd never have been born then. Mum says I never slept all night, hated boiled cabbage, and, well . . . the rest you know. I don't know if I think designer babies are a really good idea. There would be fewer people in the world like me!

But Mum really likes Velvet. She thinks she's a good influence on me because she works hard at school. I really like her because she's a nice person.

We made the timetable on Velvet's computer a few days later after school. After I'd helped her with her paper round. Velvet's mum and dad run a little post office cum grocer's shop. It's always busy because Mr and Mrs Guha are very helpful and friendly. Their flat is above the shop, and as usual, Mrs Guha had left out plenty for us to eat. I tucked into the fried cashews. Velvet had a boring bar of chocolate. Then she switched on her computer and started on the timetable.

'We'll do the bathroom one first,' she said.

It worked out as:

*Bathroom Timetable*
*Mon – Fri*
7.30 a.m. Mum.

7.45 a.m. Abby.

8 a.m. Grandma Aphrodite.

8.15 a.m. Handsome Harris.

*Sat and Sun*

By arrangement.

'Your mum starts work before you,' Velvet explained, 'and Grandma and Handsome can wait because they don't have to leave home by a set time. Grandma and Handsome can feed the animals before they have their shower, so it won't matter if they get muddy, they'll be washing afterwards anyway.'

See, sensible, like I said.

Mealtimes were organized too. Vegetarians separate from carnivores.

'Vegetarians should eat first,' said Velvet, 'because they don't like the smell of meat cooking.'

'Ah,' I said, 'but what if it's a casserole. They can take a long while to cook.'

I knew this because Grandma sometimes makes a mean beef stew that takes ages to be ready.

'Casseroles can be made the night before, AFTER everyone's eaten, and reheated the next day,' said Velvet. 'They taste better anyway, done like that, my mum says.'

There was no arguing with that. Velvet's mum is a magic cook. I love to be invited round for tea. She makes the most wonderful chicken curry, with really fluffy rice. Any time my mum makes rice we have to scrape it off the bottom of the pot with a wooden spoon, and I don't really think rice should have to be sliced.

'Finally,' said Velvet, 'a little timetable for study time.'

What! Study time! Had the girl gone completely mad?

'Your mum needs some peace and quiet to study her law books, and so do you for your homework.'

Yep, she'd gone mad all right. I usually did my homework wearing my Walkman, with one eye on the telly.

But she was right about Mum. Grandma and Handsome needed the sound on the telly turned up pretty loud and you could hear it all over the house.

'You could have your quiet time just after dinner,' Velvet went on, 'and video any programmes you might miss.'

I opened my mouth to say something, but there was nothing left to say. Velvet had got it all organized.

'I'll print out several copies of the timetable,' she said, 'then you can pin it up all over the house, so no one forgets.'

'OK,' I said. Then a thought struck. 'Velvet, do you organize everyone in your house like this?'

'Yes.'

'And does it work?'

'No.'

'Why not?'

'No one takes a blind bit of notice.'

But they did notice at 3 Pelham Way. For a start the writing on the timetables was so large that Grandma, even without her glasses, could read it at a hundred paces.

'Very impressive,' said Mum. 'Velvet's thought of everything.'

'How do you know it wasn't me?' I asked.

'Study time?' said Mum.

Fair enough.

Grandma and Handsome were impressed too.

'It's a great idea. It's good of your mum to put up with us,' said Handsome. 'We must try to make things as easy as possible for her.'

'I'll try really hard,' said Grandma.

And I know she meant it. But somehow the harder Grandma tries the more trouble she seems to get in. A bit like me really. Perhaps that's why we get on so well.

I suppose I should tell you a bit more about Handsome Harris. It's easy to describe what he's like on the outside. Big and broad and weather-beaten. You can imagine him shearing sheep or helping to build a dam, which is what he was doing to earn the money to fly over from Australia at Christmas time. And he has the biggest feet I've ever seen. I used to think my feet were big, but beside his mine are dinky. His hands are enormous too. When he picks up a cup it disappears inside his fist. Funny thing is, he has a shy smile. I'm just getting to know him myself, but it's nice having him around.

We've never had a man around the house before. First there was just Mum and me. Then Grandma Aphrodite arrived from Oz and just kind of stayed. I like having her stay with us too. She's not like anyone I've ever met before. She's completely over-the-top and down-to-earth at the same time. Weird and wonderful. She wears real crocodile-skin boots that Handsome made for her in Oz and a smelly old sheepskin jacket called Old Belle. Old Belle was their pet sheep when Grandma and Handsome lived on the sheep farm in Australia.

When Old Belle finally went belly up, Handsome made her into a jacket for Grandma. Waste not, want not, as Grandma says. Old Belle's not the most elegant jacket you've ever seen. It would never make the catwalk at a fashion show, unless it walked there on its own. But Grandma doesn't care. She doesn't care what people think of her. She always does what she thinks is right.

Like the other day, when she saw the 'Keep off the grass' and 'No ball games' notices in the park.

We were taking Benson and his doggy friends out for their daily walk – Grandma has a dog-walking business as well as Pets' Problems – and, for a change, we had gone through the park on our way to the common. We were just passing the pond with its solitary moorhen when Grandma spied the notices. She made a noise like an exploding cabbage and handed me the leads of her four dogs. Then she strode over the grass and yanked the notices out of the ground.

'Grandma, what are you doing?' I yelped. 'I'm sure you're not allowed to do that. These notices are public property.'

'Oh no, Abby,' she said, 'these notices are a

disgrace. The PARK is public property and people should be allowed to use it. What is the point of having grass if you can't enjoy walking on it!' And she marched off down the path in search of the park keeper.

I followed on as best I could with six dogs dodging round my ankles. The park keeper was in his little hut, just brewing up, when Grandma arrived. He saw the notices in Grandma's hands.

'Hello,' he said. 'Where did you find these? Bloomin' kids been pullin' them up again, I bet. I tell you, kids nowadays, they got no respect for other people's property.'

'No, the children did not pull them up,' Grandma said firmly. 'I did.'

'You did?' spluttered the park keeper, spilling tea down his jacket. 'Well you should know better at your age. That's public property, that is!'

'And so is the park,' said Grandma. 'The grass is for the public to walk on. The grass is for the children to play on, with a ball if they want.'

'We don't allow no ball games,' said the park keeper. 'That's orders.'

'Whose orders?' asked Grandma.

'Dunno. Just orders. I don't make them, Lady. I just carries them out.'

'You carry out orders that mean children have to play in the street with a ball instead of in the safety of the park? You carry out orders that mean you put children's lives at risk?'

The park keeper ran his finger round the inside of his collar and had a think.

'Look, Lady,' he said. 'Give me a break. I just work here.'

'I know, but you don't have to switch off your brain at the park gate, do you?' she asked. Then she gave him a brilliant smile. 'Now I shall be writing to the council about this matter and I shall tell them that you were very helpful. Meantime I'll take these notices away as evidence. Don't worry, I'll give you a receipt. Abby, do you have a piece of paper and a pen?'

That's how a bit of my school diary with our name and address on it came to be handed over to the park keeper. Then we carried on our way to the common. Me hanging on to six dogs and Grandma clutching two park signs to her ample bosom. Just another ordinary day in the life of Grandma!

When we finally returned the dogs to their owners and arrived home, Mum gave us one of her suspicious looks.

'Why,' she said, 'if it's not a really stupid question, are you two carrying a "Keep off the grass" and a "No ball games" sign?'

'Would you believe we found them in the road and brought them home to prevent a possible accident?' I asked.

'No, that's far too sensible for you pair,' said Mum.

'I removed them from the park as a matter of principle,' said Grandma.

'Uh oh,' grinned Handsome Harris. 'Here we go again.' He was obviously used to Grandma's little ways.

'Oh no,' said Mum and slumped into a chair. 'Your principles always get this family into trouble. What have you done now?'

Grandma took a deep breath and launched into her story.

'Good on you, Aphrodite,' said Handsome, when she'd finished. 'I think you were quite right. There are too many 'do's and 'don't's around these days.'

'Yes, like *do* pay your taxes and *don't* get involved with crooks,' snapped Mum.

It was a low blow, but Handsome just grinned. He's a good natured giant. Not easily riled.

'I think Grandma's right too,' I ventured. 'What's the point of having a park if you can't enjoy it?'

'Oh I might have known you would agree with your grandma,' sighed Mum. 'But you are right, in principle.'

'See, what did I say?' said Grandma.

'But,' went on Mum, 'there are ways of doing things, within the law. You should write to the council to complain. You don't just take the law into your own hands and yank out signs willy-nilly. Think what a state the country would be in, if everyone did that.'

Grandma had just opened her mouth to protest when the doorbell rang. Mum opened the door and the law stood there, in the form of a young WPC.

'Oh hello again,' she smiled, when she caught sight of Grandma and me behind Mum. 'I thought it must be you two when the complaint came in to the station and I saw the address. That's why I offered to come along. What *have* you been up to now?'

The police constable (whose name, we discovered, was Wendy) had met up with us before on one of Grandma's earlier escapades.

Over a cup of tea and some of Grandma's homemade scones we told her the whole story.

'We didn't steal the signs,' said Grandma.

'We gave the park keeper a receipt,' I said. 'Torn out of my school diary.'

Mum groaned.

'The signs were evidence,' said Grandma. 'You can make a citizen's arrest, can't you?' WPC Wendy nodded.

'Well, I arrested the signs as evidence for the prosecution.'

WPC Wendy smiled. Mum put her head in her hands.

The long hungry arm of the law bit

thoughtfully into her third scone. 'Perhaps,' she said, 'I could take the evidence for safe keeping, while you write to the council to state your case. That would keep matters within the law and avoid any further trouble.'

Grandma looked doubtful, and opened her mouth to protest, but Mum looked daggers at her.

'Fair enough,' said Grandma. 'But don't lose them, and I'll want a receipt.'

'No problem,' said Wendy.

Mum gave Wendy a grateful smile. 'More tea,' she said, 'and do have another scone.'

# 5

Grandma's been very busy lately with her Pets' Problems business. I suppose, like humans, animals get sicker in winter too. We had a donkey in the garden for a few days. He was very tired and just needed a rest. Probably got stressed out over Christmas doing too many nativity plays.

Handsome Harris has been a great help, though. Like Grandma, he always has to be busy. So, the moment he realized Grandma had set up the Pets' Problems business in the garden shed, and was curing sick animals using some of his old remedies, he immediately lent a hand. And a broad pair of shoulders.

There's a little alcove in the back garden where the metal bin used to be kept, before we got a wheelie bin, and Handsome fixed that up into a little house for any animal that was really poorly and needed peace and quiet. He called it the 'Quiet House'. He made a door out of old planks, and put a little window in the door, so that

Grandma could keep an eye on the sick animal inside without disturbing it. He went about his work cheerfully, whistling and singing all the time. I was fascinated by him. So were the neighbours. They were used to coming into the garden to see what animals Grandma was looking after, as well as getting some duck eggs from Quackers and Cheese and Bacon and Egg, who swam about in my old paddling pool. But now there was a gentle giant to talk to as well. Not only that, but they discovered he could mend things. Soon elderly bikes and prams and bits of motor car appeared in the back garden as well. It began to look like an old scrapyard.

Mum naturally went ballistic.

'Sorry,' said Handsome, when she came in from the back garden, fuming about the mess, to find the pair of us cleaning some spark plugs on the kitchen table. 'Sorry,' he said again and cleared the table and cleaned it up with one of Mum's new tea cloths. 'See, the thing is, folks around here don't seem to be able to fix anything for themselves. Something goes bust, they throw it away. On the sheep farm, if something broke we had to fix it. We couldn't run to the shop next door. The nearest town was half a day's drive away.'

Mum calmed down slightly.

'I understand, Handsome,' she said, 'but you can't turn the garden into a junkyard. We can't live like that. You'll have to tell people you'll go to their houses if they want something fixed.'

'OK,' said Handsome and grinned.

It was such a cheerful grin, you couldn't help grinning back. And Mum did just that. Whether she wanted to or not. There was just something about Handsome Harris. No one could stay mad at him for long. (Except the Australian mafia, that is!)

'I'll need to clear away all the junk anyway,' he said to Mum, 'before I start my next project.'

'What's that?' asked Mum.

'A proper barbie for the family.'

'But we have a proper barbie,' said Mum.

'Call that rickety thing on three legs a proper barbie?' snorted Handsome. 'I'll build you a real one, made of stone. There's a good place for it at the back of the house, out of the wind.'

Mum looked doubtful.

'Don't worry,' Handsome grinned. 'It'll look good.'

'All right.' Mum was still cautious. 'But if I don't like it, it goes.'

'No worries,' grinned Handsome.

And there were none. Handsome really knew what he was doing. Three days later, after all the old bikes and prams and bits of car engine had been repaired and removed, some stone arrived on the back of an ancient lorry and Handsome got started. I was wishing I didn't have to go to school as he started digging out the foundations for the barbie and pouring in the concrete. I wanted to lend a hand. That would be much better than doing Maths.

The ducks kept their distance at first, just waddling about, watching what went on, then curiosity got the better of them, and they were soon round about Handsome's feet, quacking their approval. Benson arrived to inspect the work in progress as well. He and Grandma had been out for their early-morning walk. He sat on the path with an alert expression on his face that meant he thought something interesting was happening. Then Grandma appeared with a cup of tea for Handsome before she went to inspect the latest inhabitant of the Quiet House. A stray cat had sneaked past everyone and had taken up residence in there to have her kittens.

Grandma had been feeding her and making sure she was well.

'I couldn't turn her out, Eva,' said Grandma, when Mum had complained that the very last thing this family needed was a pregnant cat.

But Mum's a softie underneath and she let the cat stay, on the strict understanding that Grandma found good homes for the cat and all the kittens as soon as possible after the birth.

'Of course,' said Grandma. 'If that's what you want.'

'Any news?' I asked her, as she turned away from the Quiet House.

'Not yet,' she said, 'but I don't think it'll be long.'

'I'd love to see them being born,' I said. 'I don't suppose Mum would let me stay off school today.'

'You're quite right, young lady,' said Mum, appearing at the back door. 'Now go and finish your breakfast or you'll miss the bus.'

And she collected her briefcase and went off to work muttering that 3 Pelham Way was becoming more and more like an animal hospital every day.

She was right. It was great.

I didn't miss the bus, but I was so excited at the prospect of the kittens that I inadvertently – one of my latest words – sat down beside Fishcake. I usually avoid sitting anywhere near her because she always goes on about her mum's beauty salon or about how scruffy I am. 'Don't tell me you've been standing in for a scarecrow again,' or 'Been rummaging through Oxfam's rejects?' are her usual unfunny remarks. This time it was, 'I see you spent the night in a builder's yard,' and she edged as far away from my cement-covered blazer as she could.

'No,' I said, deliberately patting my sleeve so that little clouds of cement dust flew off in her direction. 'I was just helping Handsome Harris unload bags of cement from the back of a lorry. He's going to make us a proper stone barbie.'

'Handsome Harris. What a name,' she said. 'And a barbie's nothing special. We have a huge, mobile, gas barbecue that we can wheel to any part of our large garden when we're entertaining alfresco.'

'Al Fresco? Isn't he an Italian bank robber? You should be more careful with the company you keep at your house.'

'Alfresco means in the open air, as you well know,' snapped Belinda.

Of course I did, but it was such fun winding her up.

'And didn't your mum have Al Fresco's wife in the beauty salon just before Christmas, passing counterfeit money?' I added. 'I'm sure I saw a headline in the paper that said, "Local Business 'In the Pink' Goes into the Red as Dud Tenners Discovered".'

'That's all been sorted out now,' sniffed Belinda, blushing hotly as she turned her head away and looked very pointedly out of the window.

I grinned and said no more. Belinda helped out in the beauty salon sometimes. I wondered if she'd been the one who'd accepted the dud money. We rode in unfriendly silence the rest of the way to school. We couldn't be more different, Belinda and I. She leaves home freshly pressed every morning like she just popped off the assembly line at the Barbie-doll factory. Her long blonde hair is dead straight and always smells of something edible, like strawberries or limes; never fish and chips. Belinda would never go near a fry bar. She probably reckons there are millions of calories just in the smell. I, on the other hand, love the smell and taste of fish and chips, and my red corkscrew curls smell of whatever is on special offer at the supermarket. Though I have been known to squirt myself with some of Mum's Channel 5 – or Chanel no. 5 if you want to smell nice en français – before I go to meet Andy on a Saturday.

But I'm not sure he notices. I don't suppose the perfume stands much chance against the smell of the pizzas we usually buy.

When the bus stopped at the school Andy and Velvet were waiting for me. I hopped off and hurried over to them. Belinda, head in the air, swept past us all. She secretly fancies Andy and just can't understand why he prefers me. Sometimes I don't know either, but I keep that to myself.

'Any news of the kittens?' Andy and Velvet asked.

'Not yet,' I said. 'But Grandma says it won't be long. Probably sometime this morning. I'll phone home at lunchtime, and, if they've arrived, you could come and take a peek after school, if you like.'

'Great.'

'And you can also see how the new barbie's coming along. Handsome was working on it before I left. He says that won't take long either.'

'There's always something going on at your house,' said Andy. 'It's never quiet there now.'

'Uhuh.'

'What's your mum saying about it all?' asked Velvet. She knows Mum prefers a quieter life.

'She mutters a bit,' I confessed, 'but she realizes Grandma and Handsome are just trying to help out, and she knows how much I enjoy having them around. She's going out a lot with David now too which helps to take her mind off the chaos at home.'

'That crazy idea you and your Grandma had about finding a boyfriend for your mum really worked out well,' grinned Andy.

'Yes,' I said. 'I really like David and so does Mum.'

'Have you thought that he could end up as your dad?' said Velvet.

'Oh no,' I said. 'That couldn't happen. I've already got a dad.'

And I had. Like the aliens, he was out there. Somewhere.

The kittens have arrived. I phoned home at lunchtime and Grandma said there were five of them; four male and one female. The boys all seemed to be fine and healthy, but the little girl kitten was tiny and Grandma didn't know if she would survive or not.

'We'll just have to wait and see,' she said, 'and let nature take its course.'

I told her Andy and Velvet were coming over after school to see the kittens.

'Fine,' she said. 'Handsome will pick you up.'

I told the others the news about the kittens, and it was only when I had finished that I thought, Handsome is going to pick us up? How is he going to do that? Perhaps he's borrowed Mum's car.

But he hadn't. He arrived at the school in an old truck. The same one that had delivered the old stone and the cement bags that morning.

'G'day, folks,' he grinned, when the three of us

appeared and stood open-mouthed. 'How do you like my new set of wheels? I bought the truck from the cement-bag man. He thinks it's on its last legs, but I'll soon fix it up. Now if you'd care to climb aboard, Harris's pick-up service will take you home. There's room for one more in the cabin and two in the back. Sorry it's a bit dusty.'

A bit dusty? It looked like there'd been an explosion in a talcum factory.

Andy and Velvet looked at me and grinned.

'Why don't the three of us go into the back,' said Velvet. 'It'll be fun.'

Handsome let down the tailgate and we climbed in. We sat on our rucksacks with our backs against the cabin and looked around. A small crowd had gathered to watch. Belinda and the Beelines were in the front row. They laughed and pointed.

'This must be Abby's new limo,' sneered Belinda. 'Certainly in keeping with her image.'

I opened my mouth to reply, but my words were lost as Handsome started the engine, and a cloud of black smoke belched out from the exhaust pipe. It enveloped Belinda and the Beelines. They coughed and spluttered and wiped their eyes as sooty black streaks ran down their cheeks.

'I don't think Belinda's ever been so dirty in her life,' I said happily to the others.

We roared away to a great cheer from the rest of the crowd which we acknowledged with a few royal waves. Then we rattled and bumped our way home. When we turned into Pelham Way, Grandma was already at the front gate waiting for us.

'I heard you coming miles away,' she said.

We hurled our rucksacks over the hedge into the front garden and climbed down.

'How are the kittens?' I asked.

'OK,' said Grandma, 'but don't go into the Quiet House and disturb them. Just look in the window.'

We followed the luminous dinosaur footprints – Grandma had bought them in a joke shop – round to the Pets' Problems shed then tiptoed the rest of the way to the Quiet House. We stood very quietly, taking it in turns to peep through the window. The kittens were fast asleep, curled up in a heap beside their mum. She was dozing, eyes half open. She blinked when she saw us, but didn't move.

'Oh, the kittens are lovely,' breathed Velvet.

'So tiny,' whispered Andy. 'Which one is the little girl that might not make it?'

'I don't know,' I whispered back, and felt a strange lump in my throat.

After some more oohing and aahing we trooped back to the kitchen to have some Coke and crisps.

'Which one is the little girl?' I asked Grandma. 'They were all together in a heap when we looked.'

'She's the little downy white one,' smiled Grandma.

'Will she be all right?' I hardly dared ask in case I burst into tears.

'Too early to say,' said Grandma. 'She may be little, but she's very determined. She pushes the others away and gets herself in there to feed.'

'A bit like Abby in the lunch queue when she's forgotten her sandwiches,' laughed Velvet. I threw a crisp at her.

'Have you given the kittens names yet?' asked Andy.

Grandma shook her head and handed Handsome a cup of tea. 'I thought I'd leave that up to you.'

'Perhaps we should wait and see how their personalities develop,' I said. 'Then we could name them after some of our teachers.'

'You'd want to call the good-looking one Morrison, then, wouldn't you,' giggled Velvet.

She knew I just adored my history teacher.

'And the scruffy one after Mad Max,' suggested Andy.

'What shall we call the little one then, pushing in, determined to get to the food?'

Velvet and Andy looked at each other and pretended to think hard.

'Oh that's a tricky one,' said Andy.

'Can't think what we should call her,' said Velvet.

I looked at the pair of them and light dawned.

'We are not calling her Abby,' I said. 'No way!'

At that moment the kitchen door opened and Mum arrived home with David.

'Hello everyone,' she smiled. 'I take it the kittens have arrived.'

'All five of them,' I said. 'And this lot want to call the greedy one Abby.'

'Never,' smiled David.

I knew I liked him.

'Well . . .' said Mum.

Whose side was she on?

'We'll have to find a name for the truck too,' said Handsome, finishing off his tea. 'I always give my trucks a name. I remember I had one called Speedy, and the last one was called Sparky.'

'How about Dusty?' I suggested, indicating our blazers.

'I used to have a little mare called Dusty,' said Grandma.

'Dusty it is then,' grinned Handsome.

Meantime the expression on Mum's face had gone from warm to decidedly chilly.

'You mean that broken-down old truck outside belongs here?' she gasped. 'I thought someone had abandoned it. I was about to phone the police to have it towed away.'

'Towed away? Oh no, Eva,' said Handsome, his battered face looking really concerned. 'Once I've got it fixed up, you won't know it.'

'I don't want to know it,' muttered Mum. 'This started off as a normal, ordinary household. Now we have a daft dog, a rude mynah bird, four ducks, six cats and a broken-down truck called Dusty. What next?'

'Er,' Grandma cleared her throat. 'Terrapins.'

'And terrapins in the Pets' Problems shed,' added Mum.

'Not actually . . . in the shed,' said Grandma.

'In the garden?'

'No.'

'In the paddling pool?'

'No.'

'Where then?' Mum was puzzled.

'In the bath.'

'IN THE BATH!'

And while Mum exploded like a fistful of fireworks and Grandma explained that it was only for a short time, Andy, Velvet and I shot upstairs to have a look.

'I don't remember seeing *them* on the bathroom timetable,' I giggled, as we passed it on the wall outside the bathroom door.

The terrapins were a sorry sight. So was the bath. Grandma had put in some big stones from the garden and a bit of pondweed to make them feel more at home. But they didn't look happy.

Bits of shell were dropping from them and they trailed skin like floating cobwebs. Mum, David and Grandma had come upstairs after us and the sight of the terrapins and the state of the bath did not improve Mum's temper.

'That's it,' she yelled. 'I've had enough. Get rid of these . . . *creatures* immediately.'

'But, Eva,' protested Grandma. 'I can't take these poor things back to their owner until I've found out what their problem is, and I haven't had time today what with the kittens and everything. As soon as I find out what's wrong with them . . .'

David came to the rescue. 'There's nothing wrong with them, Aphrodite,' he said. 'They're just losing their old skin and their shell. I know it looks horrible, but it's perfectly normal. I had terrapins as a child so I've seen what happens.'

'Oh great!' Grandma was delighted. 'I'll put them back in their box and take them home right away then.'

'And take the stones and the pondweed too,' said Mum. 'I want a bath.'

But Grandma was already on her way downstairs yelling, 'Start up the truck, Handsome, we can take the terrapins back right away. The good news is they're OK.'

David took Mum back downstairs to make her a calming coffee, and Andy, Velvet and I went along to my bedroom. We sat on the floor with our backs to the wall and looked at each other.

'Sorry about all the drama,' I said.

'Sorry?' said Andy. 'Don't be sorry. I love coming to your house, there's always something happening here.'

'Yes,' said Velvet. 'It's better than the soaps on the telly.'

'I know,' I said. 'Trouble is, I don't think Mum sees it that way, somehow.'

I've been thinking about my dad again. The out-there-somewhere-along-with-the-aliens dad. The one that took off when he discovered Mum was pregnant with me dad. Not really the kind of dad you'd dream of having. Sometimes, when I'm in my bed at night thinking about things, I dream up a pretend dad for myself. He's not especially tall or good-looking, but he's got a nice smile and tells terrible jokes. He's good at Maths and helps me with my homework. He's very patient and explains things so I can understand. He puts up shelves in my bedroom for all my books and takes me to the cinema. Sometimes he even takes me shopping for clothes when Mum and I have fallen out about what I should wear. He always lets me buy what I like, and tells Mum he thinks I look lovely. Even if I don't. Especially if I don't.

Perhaps you've got a dad like that. I hope so.

I hope I'll meet mine one day. At least, I think I do. I thought I wanted to know all about my dad and plucked up the courage one day to ask Mum. She gave me a shoebox full of things about him. She'd been keeping it for me because she knew one day I'd want to know. I took the box to my room and started to open it, then I stopped. I wasn't ready to find out about my real dad. I wasn't ready to give up my dream dad. I wasn't ready to know the truth. But that remark that Andy had made the other day about David becoming my dad had struck home. It hadn't really occurred to me that that might happen. Or, if it had, I had pushed it to the back of my mind. But now, here it was, right at the front.

How would I feel if David was around permanently? How would that change things? Apart from a new bathroom timetable!

For a start, I would have a stepbrother. David's son, Peter, is about my age – a few months younger. He's OK. He's heavily into computer games and communicates mostly by caveman grunts. I told him once he would grow barnacles on his bum if he didn't move around more. He just grunted and played on. I don't think he can draw like his cartoonist dad, and I don't think he likes words and books like his grandad, Charlie, who's Professor of English at the university. I like words and books so I think his grandad is great. He's an old friend of Grandma's from student days and they get on really well. But Charlie hasn't met Handsome yet. Grandma's been meaning to organize that, but she's been so busy.

Everyone's so busy these days. Grandma's up to her eyes in her Pets' Problems business as well as her dog walking. Handsome's been doing all the odd jobs around the house Mum never gets round to, as well as helping out the neighbours, and making the stone barbecue. Mum's still hoping to be made a partner in her law firm and spends a lot of her time with her law books as well as with David. And I've been busy helping Grandma and Handsome, going to school, and doing my homework as well as seeing Andy on a Saturday afternoon.

The only one who hasn't been busy is Benson. He just lies in the middle of all this activity and yawns. I think watching other people work makes him tired. He and Mortimer get on really well most of the time, except when Mortimer gets mischievous. Sometime he waits till Benson's out of the room, then, in a voice very like Mum's, he calls out, 'Benson, come here, Benson . . .'

Benson charges into the room, ears up, tail wagging, and . . . no Mum. Even worse, Mortimer calls out, 'Tea's ready, Benson!' and Benson bounds into the kitchen only to find his dish is empty. Then he slumps to the floor in a dejected heap and sighs loudly. That's when Mortimer laughs his wicked laugh. No wonder we got saddled with him when his previous owner never came back to collect him. And, try as Mum might, she still can't get Mortimer to stop saying rude words. He's taught me a few, I can tell you.

And I can tell you something else. I've decided that soon, perhaps very soon, I'm going to pluck up enough courage to open the shoebox that Mum gave me. I know it's silly to keep putting it off, and I do want to find out all about my dad. It's just that sometimes I think it's easier to have a dream dad than to find out the truth about the real one.

# 9

The new barbecue is finished and it looks fantastic. Handsome had got some old stone and some cobblestones and made the barbie out of that. It's in the shape of an H, which I suppose is appropriate, and Handsome carved his initals in the cement between two stones. Even Mum was impressed.

'It looks supberb, Handsome,' she said, reaching up to give him a peck on the cheek. 'You've done a wonderful job.'

Handsome blushed with pleasure. Grandma beamed. 'Now we'll have to have a party to christen it,' she said.

'But it's winter,' said Mum. 'Most people have barbecues in the summer.'

'Only the wimps,' said Grandma. 'And I'll do the cooking.'

'OK,' Mum agreed. She didn't like cooking much and we didn't much like what she cooked.

'It'll give me a chance to ask Prof Charlie round

to meet Handsome,' added Grandma, 'and I could also ask . . .'

'You're not inviting your jailbird friend, and that's final,' said Mum.

'Oh, Malcolm's too busy doing the rounds of the pensioners' clubs talking about crime prevention whenever he's let out of prison,' said Grandma. 'What I was going to say was perhaps we could invite some of our pensioner friends. They would enjoy a barbecued sausage or even a bit of steak, if it was tender enough, and they wore their best teeth.'

'OK,' Mum agreed, 'but no crooks.'

'What if the Australian mafia turn up?' I grinned.

'Then we'll set Benson on them,' said Grandma.

Benson opened one eye and closed it again sleepily. His tummy was tight with food and not much else mattered.

'Or we could get Mortimer to swear at them,' I suggested.

'And the ducks to nip their ankles,' said Grandma. 'They wouldn't have a hope.'

'And I suppose the kittens could lick them to death,' sighed Mum. 'No wonder people call this place Aphrodite's Ark, though Montgomery's Madhouse would be nearer it.'

But she agreed to the barbie so Grandma phoned everyone right away and arranged it for the following Saturday afternoon.

That's why I love having Grandma and Handsome to stay with us. This would never have happened if Mum and I had still been on our own.

'I've told everyone to wrap up warmly and bring an umbrella just in case,' said Grandma.

I had a sudden thought.

'What about the kittens, Grandma? There's bound to be a lot of noise with everyone chatting and laughing.'

'Oh, they'll be right,' said Grandma. 'They're not old enough to be away from their mum yet, but they can be handled now, and they have to learn to live in the world.'

'Even the little one?'

Grandma smiled. 'With a little bit of care and attention, I think she may be OK. She's put on quite a bit of weight.'

'Can we let the pensioners see them?'

'Not just see them,' said Grandma. 'I'm hoping to find good homes for them on Saturday.'

Wily old Grandma.

Next day I invited Andy and Velvet to the barbecue too.

'I'll bring some food,' said Velvet.

'What shall I bring?' asked Andy.

'Just bring yourself,' I smiled at him. 'That'll be enough.'

Andy smiled back. That special smile he has that's just for me. I could feel my ears turn pink and my legs go all wobbly. I couldn't wait for Saturday to arrive.

It took its time, but it did arrive. Eventually.

Everyone was up bright and early, scurrying about trying to get everything ready for the barbecue. Plates and cutlery were piled up in the kitchen and paper napkins were found in the tea-towel drawer. The napkins were left over from Christmas and had jolly Santas on them, but nobody would mind. Benson kept guard over the fridge. He knew there was a huge pile of sausages in there, and if one of them happened to make a big bid for freedom, he was ready to pounce.

Even Mortimer knew something was up. He kept shuffling about on his perch squawking 'Barbie barbie' and sometimes 'Bloody barbie' if he thought no one was listening.

By noon everything was ready and the first guests began to arrive. David came with Peter and Prof Charlie. Grandma introduced Charlie to Handsome and soon the two of them were deep in conversation about diesel engines.

Then the pensioners arrived.

Mrs Polanski hobbled in carrying a large Polish sausage.

'Just in case you run out of food,' she said. 'Cut it up small and serve them all.'

Miss Flack brought Mum a beautiful cushion she'd made and embroidered with an E for Eva. She's a wizard with a needle.

Major Knotts brought a little brandy.

'Purely medicinal,' he winked. 'Just to keep out the cold.'

And Mrs Hobbs brought Mr Hobbs, who brought his toy train with him.

'He always loved trains when he was a little boy,' she said, 'and likes to keep it beside him now.'

Finally Velvet arrived with the biggest bowl of pakora you ever saw. She immediately handed it round.

'It's freshly made. Mum says to eat it while it's still warm,' she said.

No one needed to be told twice.

'Leave room for the rest,' called Handsome, as he expertly flipped over the sausages and steaks.

Fortunately the weather was mild and dry and everyone wandered round the garden with their rolls filled with steak and sausages. Only Mrs Polanski with her bad feet sat just inside the back door on a comfy chair. Grandma tucked an old blanket round her legs to keep her warm. The blanket was Benson's and smelled a bit. Mrs Polanski didn't mind – Benson used to be her dog when she was more able to look after him.

Then Grandma brought out the kittens and handed them round. There was even more oohing and aahing than we had done.

'When will they be ready to leave their mother?' everyone wanted to know.

'Soon,' said Grandma, giving me a wink. 'I'll let you know.'

The barbie was a great success in more ways than one. Prof Charlie asked Handsome if he could come over to his house and take a look at his car which had an annoying rattle. Mrs Polanski asked him to fix her leaking roof. Miss Flack was having problems with a smelly drain and Major Knotts had a table with a wobbly leg.

'My breakfast keeps sliding on to my lap,' he said.

'Of course, we'll pay you, Handsome,' everyone insisted. 'You must set yourself up in business, just like Aphrodite.'

'And now you've got the truck in good working order,' said Prof Charlie, 'you can travel further afield to do business.'

So Handsome Harris' Helping Hands business was born.

'I could paint four Hs on the side of the truck,' grinned Handsome.

'It's a great idea,' said Mum. 'But you will keep a record of all your business and pay your taxes. I don't want any more crooks around here.'

'No worries,' grinned Handsome.

And Grandma had found homes for the kittens. I was a little bit sad when she told us about it later. I'd got used to hurrying home from school to see them.

'Mrs Polanski will take the mother cat,' said

Grandma, 'once the cat's been neutered. We don't want her having any more kittens. Miss Flack wants the little stripy one. Major Knotts has got some mice in his attic and wouldn't mind the biggest black kitten, and Mr and Mrs Hobbs are going to have one each.'

I did a mental calculation and even with my numeracy bypass I knew that still left one kitten.

'What about the littlest one?' I said.

'Well, I didn't want to promise her to anyone,' said Grandma, 'just in case she's still a little weak. It would be very upsetting for one of the old folks if the kitten died.'

'Quite right,' said Mum. 'We wouldn't want that.'

'Can we keep her then, if we can't give her away? We couldn't possibly put her to sleep . . .' I looked at Mum.

'No,' she said. 'We couldn't possibly do that.'

'So?'

'So, what are you going to call her?' sighed Mum.

'Dunno,' I said and gave her a hug.

'Strange name for a cat.'

'Listen,' I grinned. 'I do the jokes.'

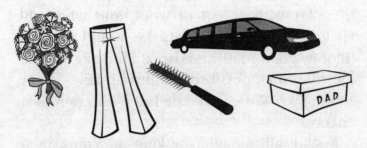

I called the kitten Rosie, because she has the cutest little pink nose. After a while the kittens were able to leave their mother and they were all shipped off to their new homes. Rosie left the Quiet House and came to live with us. Benson and Mortimer were a bit huffy at first. Here was a stranger on their territory. Benson lay right in front of the fire and put on his this-is-my-place-and-I'm-not-moving-for-anyone expression, while Mortimer kept a beady eye on the kitten at all times. Although she was very tiny, she was still a cat, and Mortimer was very wary of cats. He sat on his perch muttering, 'Look out, look out, a cat's about.'

But, before long, Rosie had them both eating out of her tiny paw. She tiptoed daintily over to Benson and lifted her little pink nose to his big black one. Then she gave a little squeak and settled down between his paws and went to sleep. Benson, big softie that he is, immediately fell in love, and from then on the pair of them were best friends. It took Mortimer a little while longer to accept Rosie, but he loved to watch her play with a ball of wool, and when she flicked it under the sofa he would squawk, 'Bloody good goal!' and dance a little jig to some internal tune, possibly in a mynah key – sorry, rotten joke. Rosie would do her trick again as an encore.

Best of all, though, she kept me company in my room at night. She wasn't supposed to. She was supposed to be in her little basket beside Benson's big basket, beside the central heating boiler in the kitchen. But Benson was never there because he kept guard outside Mum's bedroom door; inside if he could manage it. So, Rosie, as soon as she was big and strong enough to climb the stairs, came too.

She gave me the fright of my life the first time she did this. I wakened up in the middle of the night and found myself nose to nose with a kitten. She had been sitting very still on top of my duvet, watching me sleep. Now she sleeps at the foot of my bed on an old pink cot blanket that used to be mine. Mum goes on and on about how unhygienic it is, but Grandma said, 'You worry too much, Eva, old Belle used to share our bedroom and it didn't do Handsome and me any harm – apart from the twitch, the limp and the gniyas sgniht sdrawkcab.'

'What?'

'Saying things backwards.'

'You're a lunatic,' said Mum. 'You shouldn't be allowed out on your own. It's a wonder I grew up so normal.'

Grandma just snorted, and I got to have Rosie in my bedroom. She's brilliant; soft and cuddly and a very good listener. She now knows all about the teachers at Cosgrove High and shakes her head in disgust when I tell her about Belinda and the Beelines. She agrees with me that Velvet's a really good friend and that Andy is just plain gorgeous. She would fancy him too if he had four paws and a tail. And I whispered to her about my dad and the shoebox full of things about him that Mum had given me. I even brought it down from the top of my wardrobe and showed it to her.

'But I haven't opened it yet,' I told her.

Rosie looked at me with her head on one side, then did a funny thing. She started pawing at the Sellotape round the lid of the box, and the bit that I had already peeled back and stuck down again (when I got too scared to open the box) came away.

I gave a little gasp. If Ms Tickle was here, she would say it was a sign, I thought. Ms Tickle was a clairvoyant friend of Grandma's. Well, I couldn't see into the future, but I could look into the past, if I opened up the box. I took a deep breath, peeled away the rest of the Sellotape and lifted off the lid.

The box held mainly letters and photographs. I spread them out on my bed and looked at them. There were several photos of my dad as a boy. I knew it was him because he had the same knobbly knees as me and the same wiry red hair. Later photos showed him with sideburns and flares. He obviously had my fashion sense too. Then there were photos of him and Mum together. One at the funfair eating candy floss, one beside a beat-up old car painted purple, and one showing them all dressed up and formal at a wedding.

There was a photo of their own wedding too. I looked at that one really closely. Mum looked very young in a short white dress with flowers in her hair. Dad, my dad – and that felt funny to even think never mind say – wore burgundy velvet trousers and a pink frilly shirt. I couldn't believe it; the colours were the same as the outfit I'd worn to the school Christmas disco. I stared at the photos for ages. This was my dad. Not my dream dad. My real dad. And I looked like him. I had his tall lanky shape and his unruly hair.

I could feel tears pricking behind my eyelids. I rubbed them away with the back of my hand. I looked round for Rosie and found her curled up inside the box. I lifted her out and examined the rest of the contents. There was a Valentine's card with a silly rhyme inside that my dad had sent to my mum. Funny birthday cards they had sent to each other. There was my dad's cycling proficiency certificate and several certificates for swimming, along with a few Boy-Scout badges with bits of thread round the edges. Crazily, I wondered what had happened to the Scout shirt they had been cut from. There was a Scout Entertainer's badge stuck inside a joke book. I read some of the jokes, they were terrible, e.g.:

'*How do you make anti-freeze?*'
'*Stick her in the fridge.*'

I was just groaning at that joke when something in my brain went PING and I looked back at the wedding photograph of mum and dad. There were some other people in the background that I obviously didn't recognize. But it was a wedding photo. Could they be relatives? Perhaps I had an auntie that I didn't know about, or an uncle, or cousins even.

I would have to talk to Mum. She said, when she gave me the box, that she would answer any questions that I had. Any questions? There were so many, I didn't know where to start. But I had made a start by opening the box.

'Thanks, Rosie,' I said, stroking her delicate little ears. 'You helped me do it.'

Rosie gave an enormous yawn, showing off her little pointy teeth. I went to the bathroom and cleaned my caged ones, came back to my room and climbed into bed. Then, in a fold of my duvet,

I noticed a letter from the box I had missed. It had funny watermark splashes on the outside of the envelope. I opened up the single page and read it. It was the letter to my mum from my dad telling her he was leaving, that he couldn't cope with the responsibility of a family. I guess the watermark splashes were my mum's tears. My own tears, which had been threatening since I opened the box, spilled out, ran down my cheeks and soaked my pillow. My insides heaved and I cried and cried. Rosie abandoned the pink cot blanket at the foot of my bed and came and sat on my pillow. Her little rough tongue licked away the salty tears on my cheek.

'Oh Rosie,' I blubbed. 'Poor Mum.'

Rosie said nothing, just settled down to sleep next to me. I stroked her head for a bit then did something I haven't done since I was tiny. I put my thumb in my mouth, and, comforted, I fell asleep.

# 11

I've been helping Handsome Harris round the house. He's already fixed all the wobbly shelves in the kitchen and put up new ones. The washing machine has stopped juddering across the kitchen floor and pinning Mum to the wall, and the front door has lost its squeak. The back garden has been transformed too. Handsome has laid a proper concrete path around the sides so Grandma doesn't have to trail across the muddy grass to get to the Pets' Problems shed, and he's built neat little wooden enclosures where, during the day, Grandma can put the animals she's looking after. When the weather improves, he's even going to dig out a proper pond for the ducks.

I, of course, have been his first mate/ apprentice/gofer. I can now hammer in a straight nail, mix cement – three parts sand to one part cement – and change the washer on a tap. When Handsome had finished fixing up his old truck

Andy and I helped give Dusty a coat of paint. I even stencilled four Hs on the side. I'm no Picasso, but Mad Max would have been proud of me. The house and the garden and the truck were looking pretty good and Mum was very pleased. Handsome really did try hard to be helpful. Perhaps too hard. Just when Mum was happy with everything neat and tidy, Handsome decided to rewire the house.

'The wiring's dangerous, Eva,' he said. 'The circuits are overloaded. There are too many appliances coming off the one feed.'

What???

Mum put on an intelligent expression and pretended she knew what he meant. I do the same thing in Maths.

'I see,' she said.

'But don't worry,' said Handsome. 'I can do it, no problem.'

Mum frowned. 'How long will rewiring take?'

'Not long,' said Handsome, 'it's not such a big job,' and he went off to buy the materials he needed. He just loved to have a project.

I couldn't wait to get back from school to give him a hand. I think I may well be a plumber/joiner/handyperson when I grow up. I wonder if you need to pass your Maths exam for that.

I could hear the hammering and banging as I came up the garden path that afternoon. The rewiring had obviously started. I opened the front door and . . . what a mess! Nothing was where it should have been. The sitting-room furniture was piled up in the middle of the floor, the kitchen appliances were in a muddle in the kitchen, and, upstairs in my bedroom, my bed was standing on its end. Rosie was crouched on top of my wardrobe where she thought it was safe. The hammering and banging was coming from Mum's room. I opened the door cautiously and looked in. Handsome was on his knees ripping wires out of a channel he had opened up in the wall.

'Hi, Abby,' he said. 'Had a busy day?'

'Not as busy as you,' I said.

'Yeah,' he grinned. 'It always looks terrible at the start, but it'll be right soon enough.'

I believed him, but would Mum?

Silly question.

She came back from work, staggering under a huge pile of books, and dropped them where the hall table should have been. They fell on her toe.

'Ow! What's happened to my house?'

We could hear the yell upstairs. If there happened to be a man on the moon at that moment, he would have heard it too. Even little green men on Mars in the middle of eating their Earth bars would have stopped and said, 'There is definitely something out there.'

I dropped the plug I was helping Handsome wire up and he gave me a little half smile.

'I think your mum's home,' he said.

Mum came thundering upstairs like an angry rhino whose dinner had just escaped and threw open her bedroom door. Handsome and I stood there like two kids caught with their fingers in the cookie jar.

'What is this . . . mess?'

'Just the start of the rewiring, Eva,' soothed Handsome. 'I know it looks bad just now, but it'll soon be much better.'

'And you can't make an omelette without breaking eggs,' said Grandma, coming up the stairs behind Mum. She was holding several interesting-looking carrier bags.

'I knew cooking might be difficult this evening so I went out and bought us some takeaways. Come and eat, Eva, before you burst your knicker elastic!'

'Eat,' stormed Mum. 'Is that your answer to everything?'

'Pretty much,' smiled Grandma. 'If you're going to holler and yell, best do it on a full stomach. I bought your favourite bean sprouts,' she added slyly. 'Don't let them get cold.'

We all trooped down to the sitting room, or the standing room as it now was.

'Park your bum wherever you can,' said Grandma, 'and tuck in.'

The bean sprouts calmed Mum down a little. 'I didn't realize there would be so much mess,' she muttered.

'We'll soon get it cleared up,' said Handsome. 'And the house will be much safer, which is the important thing.'

'We've put your computer back in its corner, so you can get on with your work,' I said.

'Good. I've got a pile of stuff on disk to put into it tonight.' And she finished off her bean sprouts and went upstairs.

The rest of us gave a sigh of relief and were just giving the remnants of the takeaway to Benson, who'd been waiting patiently, when there was a bang and a yell.

We all rushed upstairs.

Mum's face was stony. 'Someone,' she said, 'messed about with the plug on my computer and I have just lost a day's work.'

'Sorry, Eva,' said Handsome. 'I'll see if I can fix it.'

But Mum would have none of it. She ordered us all out and banged the door behind us.

'Handsome,' I whispered. 'Wasn't that the plug I was fixing?'

'Nah,' he said. 'Couldn't have been.' And he grinned at me, a big face-splitting grin.

I grinned back. He really was a nice man.

# 12

It was time to have a long talk to Mum about men. Men in general and one in particular, my dad. I had gathered myself together enough to be able to talk about him without blubbing. I hoped.

The rewiring of the house was nearly finished and Grandma and Handsome had sent Mum and me to the movies so they could get on with the clearing up in peace. But, when we got to the cinema, there was an enormous queue. Mum hates queuing so we went to a pizza place instead. Mum had the veggie platter while I had a pizza with everything on top. It was early evening and the restaurant was quiet, so between mouthfuls of pizza I mumbled, 'I finally opened the shoebox you gave me.'

'Uhuh,' Mum twisted some carrot strands round her fork.

'And I do have some questions.'

'Uhuh.'

Amazing how inarticulate lawyers can be sometimes.

'You said you would answer them.'

'Yes,' said Mum. She stopped tormenting the carrot and put it safely back among her lettuce.

'How old were you when you got married?'

'Twenty. I was still at law school.'

'And my dad?'

'About the same age. He was at drama school.'

'Do you mean he's an actor now? Will I have seen him on the telly?' I squeaked.

Mum shook her head. 'He dropped out of drama school. Didn't finish his course. He wasn't good at finishing anything. He got bored easily.'

'Did he get bored with you?'

It wasn't a very kind question, but it just popped out.

'He got bored with being married, I think,' said Mum. 'Then, the thought of bringing up a child . . . well, it was just too much responsibility.'

'I see.'

I didn't really, but I would think about it later. Then I remembered about the wedding photograph.

'Does he have brothers and sisters?'

'One sister. She went abroad. I'm not sure where.'

'So, I could have cousins.'

'Possibly.'

'You didn't keep in touch with any of the family?'

'No.'

'And they didn't keep in touch with you, even to ask about me?'

Mum poked the carrot again.

'Your dad's mum died when he was a teenager, and he didn't tell his father I was pregnant. After he walked out, I didn't either. I didn't want anything to do with any of the family. Maybe I was wrong. I don't know.'

Help. Mum usually knew everything.

I tried some easier questions.

'Do I look like my dad?'

'Yes.'

'Do I act like him?'

'Sometimes.'

'Is that why you go on so much about homework and exams?'

'Probably, and because I'm a real nag,' she smiled.

I smiled back. 'You should have told me.'

'Yes.'

I concentrated on my pizza for a while, thinking about Mum and Dad being married and things not working out. Then another question popped out.

'Are you really serious about David?'

Mum blushed to the roots of her hair.

'Yes,' she mumbled.

'Is he serious about you?'

'I think so.'

'So?'

'So I don't know,' said Mum. 'I've had one bad experience, I don't know if I want to risk another.'

'Uhuh.' I sucked the last of my Coke making that horrible noise with the straw.

'Would you like another Coke?' asked Mum, taking the hint.

'Please,' I said, and while she went to get it I had a bit of a think.

'All men aren't the same, though, are they?' I asked her when she came back. 'Just because my dad was immature doesn't mean they're all like that. Look at Handsome and Charlie. They're really nice, and my history teacher's got three kids and he's lovely.'

Mum laughed. 'Pity I can't marry him then, isn't it?'

Marry? Who said anything about marriage? Did I say anything about marriage? I don't think so. I said 'serious', that was all. I opened my mouth then shut it again. I had probably asked enough questions for the moment.

# 13

School assembly day. I like assemblies, they break up the morning and give you something else to talk about. Mrs Jackson doesn't like assemblies. She doesn't like having to try to get us to concentrate after them.

And, today there was big news.

You can always tell when Mr Doig has big news, because he tells you he has an important announcement to make, then he talks about everything else instead. He does all the minor stuff about litter in the playground etc. first, and keeps us on tenterhooks till the end. So . . .

There's to be a school talent contest for charity.

The school is involved in raising money for a playroom in the local hospital and Mr Doig had come up with the idea of a talent contest.

'I know there is a lot of talent in this school,' he said, 'so don't be shy. A notice will come round the classes. Put your name down if you're interested, and I'll get back to you later with further details.'

A talent competition! Ripples of surprise ran round the hall and people pulled WOW! faces.

Then Marty Foreman put up his hand.

'Yes, Marty?' Mr Doig didn't look surprised. Marty asks even more questions than I do.

'Will the teachers be in the talent contest too?'

Mr Doig raised his eyebrows. He obviously hadn't thought of that. Then he smiled, a rather mischievous smile. 'I don't see why not,' he said.

There was an even bigger ripple of surprise and a few concerned looks from the teachers. Good old Marty. This could be fun. Then the worry set in. What could I do? What talent did I have? I wasn't much good at singing, except in the bath, along with my Walkman. Reciting poetry wearing a dental brathe ith juss not on, and dancing, with my two large left feet, was just not possible.

Not that I hadn't tried. Mum took me to dancing lessons when I was little, but, after a few weeks, the teacher asked Mum to remove me from the class. Apparently I kept falling over my feet and knocking everyone else down too. The entire class of three-year-olds went down like a row of dominoes and went home with bruises. Their mothers complained. I probably didn't suit the pink tutu anyway. So what could I do? It was a problem.

Belinda Fishcake, however, had no such problem.

'I shall just do one of my pop songs,' she said.

'Great, Belinda. We'll be your backing group. If you want us that is,' gushed the Beelines. Vomit. Vomit.

Belinda smiled her superior smile.

'I'll organize some auditions for that shortly,' she said, 'and let you know.'

Plonker.

'What are you going to do?' I asked Velvet on our way back from the main building to Stalag 3.

'Me?' squeaked Velvet. 'I'm not going to do anything. I'm not going up on stage. Don't be ridiculous!'

Of course, she wouldn't. I'd forgotten Velvet was so shy. She blushes furiously if a boy even smiles at her.

'I'll help behind the scenes,' she said. 'Sell programmes, put out chairs, whatever, but wild horses wouldn't get me up on that stage.'

Strange how different people are. Wild horses wouldn't keep me off.

I told Mum and Grandma and Handsome all about the contest when I got home. They all said the same thing. 'What will you do?'

Not, you'll note, 'Are you going to enter?' They know me so well.

'I don't know what I'll do,' I said. 'I'm not much good at singing.'

Mum agreed. Rather too readily, I thought.

Grandma said, 'I used to be in a pop group way back in the sixties.'

Now why didn't that surprise me?

'I think we should listen to you first,' said Grandma. 'I've got my old guitar up in my trunk in the attic, I'll go and get it and you can give us a song.'

Grandma disappeared upstairs. We heard the clang of the loft ladder being pulled down then, after some bangings and clatterings, she appeared back downstairs with her old guitar. Some restringing and retuning was necessary, then the guitar was ready.

'Your grandma used to play for us out on the sheep farm,' beamed Handsome. 'She was great.'

Grandma smiled back at him. They really did like each other, this pair.

Grandma struck up a chord.

'Right, what will you sing, Abby? Try something simple to begin with.'

'Sing "Ten Green Bottles",' said Handsome. 'That was one of my favourites when I was a boy.'

'Ten Green Bottles'? He must have been a boy when Adam was a lad.

I cleared my throat and began.

'*Ten green bottles hanging on the wall*
*Ten green bottles hanging on the wall*
*But if one green bottle should accidentally fall . . .*'

I sang my heart out, but something was wrong.

Grandma was playing louder and louder, Mortimer was squawking, 'Give us a break! Give us a break!', and Benson had crawled underneath the sofa, put his paws over his ears and was howling fit to burst. Meanwhile Mum and Handsome couldn't stop laughing. Were they trying to tell me something?

# 14

Apparently I don't have a very good singing voice. Mum made this perfectly plain when she gasped out between fits of laughter, 'Abby, that's terrible. Really terrible.'

'Well, don't mince your words,' I said. 'Don't worry about hurting my feelings. Just say what you think!'

Handsome was no better. He wiped his eyes with the sleeve of his old jersey.

'Sorry to laugh, Abby, but your mum's right. That voice of yours could peel paint.'

'Peel paint. Peel paint,' squawked Mortimer, dancing about on his perch. Benson crawled out from underneath the sofa wagging his tail.

'Perhaps I just need to warm up some more,' I said. 'It sounds much better when I'm in the bath.'

'That's because you've got your earphones on and can't hear it,' said Mum.

She really was being very unhelpful.

'Well, that's it then,' I huffed. 'I can't dance or recite poetry and I don't know any jokes.' I thought briefly of my dad's old joke book up in the shoebox, but if I told any of those I'd be run out of town. 'I'll just have to give up the idea.'

'Give up? Give up?' said Grandma. 'I'll pretend I didn't hear that.'

'So, do you think if I practised, Grandma?'

'Nope,' Grandma shook her head. 'You have to face it, Abby. You're tone deaf. I don't think you've a musical note in your body. Certainly not one that comes out of your mouth.'

Now I was really annoyed. Grandma is usually an ally.

'But . . .' she smiled, before I could storm off in high dudgeon . . . hang about, what exactly is a dudgeon? A badly designed dungeon? And if there's a high dudgeon, can you get a low one? Answers on a postcard please.

'. . . But there is another possibility.'

'What?' I asked suspiciously.

'What happened when you started to sing?'

'Everybody laughed,' I muttered.

'Exactly,' said Grandma, 'because it was so awful, it was funny. Now if we could work up a little comedy act with you singing and me playing and Benson and Mortimer joining in like they did, you'd be a smash hit.'

A smash hit. I liked the sound of that. My

over-fertile imagination soared. I could see my name in lights. BIG lights outside a HUGE theatre.

ABBY MONTGOMERY
And her World Famous Comedy Team
Starring in the Brand New Smash Hit
HIGH DUDGEON

'But we will need to practise,' I came down to earth to hear Grandma say.

'Where?' asked Mum. 'There's no room to do anything in this house, and I am trying to work some of the time.'

'You could always go over to David's,' said Grandma slyly.

'Hmm,' Mum was non-committal, though it was plain she liked the idea.

'Right,' I said. 'Should I start to practise my singing now?'

'No,' everyone said. Rather too quickly, I thought.

'Your singing's perfect the way it is,' said Grandma. 'I just have to devise a little routine to get Benson and Mortimer more involved, then we'll practise that.'

'What shall *I* do?'

'Your homework,' suggested Mum.

Spoilsport.

# 15

Teachers are definitely from another planet. How can they announce something like the talent contest then expect us to concentrate on school work?

'Ce n'est pas possible,' as my French teacher, Mr Powers, always says when he looks at my homework. Hey! That's another idea for the little routine Grandma and I are working up. Perhaps I could sing one of my songs in French. 'Sur le Pont d'Avignon', perhaps. I could wear a stripy jumper and a little black beret and have a string of onions round my neck.

Trouble is, I don't know if Benson can howl in French – though I'm sure Mortimer knows some rude French words. Did you know that the bridge at Avignon only goes halfway across the river? Strange but true.

Belinda and the Beelines have commandeered Stalag 3 to practise their song. They spend every break tra-laaing and da-deeing, and working out their dance routines, till everyone's fed up with it. Well, I am anyway.

Andy and Velvet are really enthusiastic about my comedy routine. I haven't told anyone else as I want it to come as a complete surprise at the audition. Andy has offered to look after the props and do any clearing up, just in case Mortimer or Benson should get too excited and have a little 'accident'. I think Grandma should be all right. Velvet has volunteered to act as prompt, just in case I get stage fright and forget my lines.

Everyone is so thrilled about the contest and can talk about little else. The big questions are, though, which teachers will enter and what will they do? There's a rumour going round that Mrs Jackson is a secret line dancer and does her weekend shopping in a stetson and cowboy boots, and that Mr Soames does conjuring tricks for charity in his spare time, but I don't know if that's true.

It's funny, but you don't think of teachers as having another life outside school, do you? You just expect them to be there, at the front of the classroom, where you left them the day before. Like they had spent all night in the cupboard along with the Maths books or the Bunsen burners, and just popped out again next day to teach you a few more facts and figures. It's hard to imagine them as a mum or a dad.

Andy's mum's a teacher and he moans that he

never gets to skip his homework. But I've been round at his house and met his mum, and she seems remarkably normal for a teacher. She complains about the same things my mum does: untidy bedrooms, mugs left lying all round the house and dirty socks hiding under the bed. But she makes a really good chocolate cake and wonderful chewy meringues, so she can't be all bad.

She also sits at night and marks piles of homework. Perhaps she'd rather be doing something else. Perhaps we could come to some arrangement with the teachers. If they didn't give us any homework, we wouldn't do any, and they wouldn't have to mark it. Then we could all get on with our line dancing, meringue making, telly watching etc. Simple really. My mind must be more brilliant than I thought.

Am I giving you the impression that I don't like homework much? Actually I don't mind some of it, but Velvet positively loves all of it. She always does hers neatly and well. But she likes working hard and passing exams. She going to be a brilliant brain surgeon or rocket scientist or world leader some day. I can just tell somehow. Perhaps I am going to be a clairvoyant like Ms Tickle says. She says I'm a very sensitive person. I told Mum this and she snorted and said I was about as sensitive as a lavatory brush. I thought this was very unkind, and unfair to lavatory brushes. If they ever get to hear of it they'll probably all need counselling.

Perhaps it's surprising that Velvet and I are such good friends, because we're so unalike. Perhaps it's the attraction of opposites. Or perhaps we just like each other.

Anyway, no one's doing much work in school at the moment, apart from Velvet, and even the teachers can be spotted in corners, chatting and giggling. They fall silent when we approach. I bet they're talking about the talent contest. Maybe they're more like us than I thought. Maybe they're not from another planet after all. BIG maybe.

# 16

It was Friday and I came home thinking, Yippee! No school for two whole days and a lie-in tomorrow.

How wrong can one girl be?

When Grandma came back from her dog walking, she had news.

'I had a phone call from a newspaper reporter today,' she said. 'She's heard all about the Pets' Problems business and how people round here call this place Aphrodite's Ark, and she wants to come and interview me.'

'Cool,' I said. I was impressed.

'She said it would make a splendid feature for the local paper,' said Grandma.

'When's she coming?' I asked.

'Tomorrow morning.'

There goes the lie-in, I thought. I would have to be up and about for several reasons. One, because I am Grandma's number one assistant with the animals and might be required to give the reporter some information. Two, because I like to use big words and might possibly chat to the reporter about journalism as a career. And three, because I am just plain nosy.

But, at least I could laze about tonight in front of the telly.

No chance.

'You mean there's a reporter coming here tomorrow morning,' said Mum, when Grandma told her the story.

'Uhuh,' said Grandma.

'Well, we'd better get started right after dinner, then,' said Mum.

'Started on what?' said Grandma.

'Cleaning this house,' said Mum. 'I don't want it all over the paper that we have a dirty house.'

'But we don't,' said Grandma. 'It's a bit untidy sometimes, but so is everyone else's. That's normal.'

'And she's not coming to see the house,' I said. 'She's coming to chat about the animals.' But Mum would have none of it.

Bang went the telly watching. After dinner, the big clean-up began. Handsome tried to sneak out of it by going outside to see the animals, but Mum was ready for him and sent him out there with a mop and a duster as well. I was on polishing detail, Grandma got the hoovering to do and Mum washed the inside of the windows.

Crazy or what.

I went to bed exhausted. And I had to be up early.

Mum inspected me when I came downstairs the next morning.

'Go back up and put on your best jeans,' she said. 'You don't want to look scruffy for the photographs.'

Photographs! It was worse than when the photographers came to the school. Mum always made sure I left for school extra clean and tidy on that day, but despite her best efforts, all my school photos showed me with my tie round my ear, my socks at half-mast and a dopey expression on my face.

'Do you do it deliberately?' Mum always asked when I brought the awful photograph home.

'No,' I said. 'It's a gift.'

So I went upstairs, put on my best jeans and jumper, and came back downstairs and waited and waited. Grandma came back with Benson and waited and waited. When the reporter eventually arrived she was wearing old jeans and a scruffy T-shirt under her anorak. 'Sorry I'm late,' she said. 'I like a bit of a lie-in on a Saturday.'

Her name was Mandy and she was very friendly. If she noticed the sparkling windows, the clean carpets and the beautifully polished furniture, she didn't say. But she was interested in the animals and about all of Grandma's old remedies. She was also very interested to hear

Grandma's views about the notices in the park and about how Grandma hadn't heard back from the council yet, despite several letters and phone calls.

So she wrote about that in her article too.

Mum was mortified when she saw it in the newspaper.

'How do you think it looks to people?' she said. 'Your daughter is a lawyer and you take the law into your own hands.'

'I think it looks like I'm a concerned citizen,' shrugged Grandma, and said no more.

She didn't have to. The following week, the letters page in the paper was full of letters from other concerned citizens supporting Grandma, and saying she was quite right to do what she had done, and what was the council going to do about it?

A few days later Grandma finally got a letter from the council.

It said they appreciated her point of view and that in future the notices would only appear on bits of the park where new grass needed time to grow. The other areas would be free for people to walk on or children to play.

Grandma showed the letter to Mum.

Mum shook her head in disbelief. 'How do you manage it?' she said.

'It's a gift,' grinned Grandma.

That must be who I get it from.

The audition for the talent contest is today. I am so excited. I checked with Mrs Jackson about Grandma and the pets taking part, and she asked Mr Doig about it.

'Great idea,' he said. 'We want to encourage links with the home and the community and Grandma Aphrodite came to speak to our pupils a few months ago about life in the sixties, didn't she? She's obviously a strong supporter of the school and that's just what we want. Of course she can take part.'

So Grandma and Mortimer and Benson were in.

The auditions took place in the main hall after school. I met Grandma at the door and took Mortimer's cage from her while she carried in her guitar and had Benson trot to heel.

The hall seemed different somehow from when we're in there for assembly, just as it seemed different when we were in there for the school disco. I wonder how that happens. I can feel a new theory coming on. I already have the Abigail Montgomery Theory of Time i.e. it slows down or speeds up depending on what you are doing. Now I shall have the Abigail Montgomery Theory of Place i.e. the feeling of a place changes depending upon the activity carried out there. I think that sounds pretty impressive to begin with.

I'm sure I can feel my brain expanding as my brain cells get to work. I wonder if brain cells get lazy if you don't use them. Like Mum mutters about the size of her bum if she doesn't go to the gym – which she doesn't very often. I wonder if brain cells can get flabby too? I wonder if they make New Year resolutions to be more intelligent in the future? Perhaps they perk themselves up by doing press-ups. Except, can you do press-ups if you don't have any arms or legs? Perhaps they do bounce-ups instead. I'll ask my science teacher, Mr Burnett, about it – though he'll probably think I'm a nutter as usual.

There were quite a few people in the hall. Those who were there to audition, plus Mr Doig and teachers from the Music and Drama departments who were there to give the thumbs-up or down to the performers. Mr Doig greeted Grandma with a hearty handshake. Grandma returned it. Mr Doig winced.

'How nice to meet you, Mrs Harris,' he boomed. 'Abby's told us so much about you, and it's good of you to take part in our talent competition. And this must be Benson and Mortimer.'

'Hello, Mortimer,' he said to Benson.

Benson gave him the look he usually reserves for poncy-smelling poodles.

'Hello, Benson,' he said to Mortimer.

'Plonker,' squawked Mortimer.

Oops. Mortimer had learned that one from me.

'What interesting pets,' said Mr Doig, which I think is head-teacher speak for 'get them out of here'.

Someone else had the same idea.

'I don't think it's right,' said Fishcake, sidling up behind me, 'that you should be allowed to audition with your grandma and animals. This contest should just be for humans.'

'Well, you've got the Beelines backing you,' I said, 'and rumour has it they're clones.'

'Hmmph,' said Belinda and flounced off. She does that flouncing bit so well.

The auditions began and there was a fair mixture of talent. There were quite a few pop singers. Some good, some bad, and all of them better than me. There was a juggler who was really boring, but doing all right till he dropped one of his balls and it rolled off the stage. Benson pounced on it and ran round the hall. I gave chase and Mortimer squawked 'Go, Benson, go!' Benson thought this was a great new game. Some other competitors and teachers joined in and tried to head Benson off. He thought this was an even better game and dodged here and there, avoiding everyone. Once he dropped the ball and flicked it with a lazy paw through Mr Doig's legs before retrieving it on the other side. Given half a chance that dog could play for the national team.

Eventually Grandma, who been enjoying the spectacle, though not the juggler, called, 'Benson, heel!'

Benson immediately trotted over to her.

Grandma pointed to the stage. 'Give back the ball.'

Benson galloped up on to the stage and dropped the ball at the juggler's feet. Then he faced the audience and wagged his tail. I'm sure he was waiting for a round of applause.

Most people laughed. It had been a great chase. But Belinda and the Beelines were furious because Benson was the centre of attention. The juggler wasn't too pleased either when he picked up his ball and found it all wet and slobbery. Benson does tend to dribble a bit when he gets excited.

Belinda and the Beelines were next up on stage. The Beelines stood in a semi-circle behind Belinda while she went to the front of the stage and gave the audience the benefit of her full thirty-two-teeth smile.

'Today,' she smiled, 'I'm going to sing a popular number already in the charts, but you may want to know that I am in the process of writing my own songs and that one day I intend to have my own record label as well as a modelling career.'

She really was modest to a fault, that girl.

The audience fell silent as Belinda began. I had to admit that all the practising in Stalag 3 had paid off and she really didn't sound too bad at all. Though Mortimer didn't think so.

'Bloody racket. Bloody racket,' he managed to squawk before Grandma threw Old Belle over his cage to shut him up.

Then it was our turn. Grandma rescued her jacket from the cage and Mortimer woke up. 'G'day all,' he said in his best Ozzie accent.

We trooped up on to the stage. Grandma perched on the end of an old school table with her guitar. Mortimer, now out of his cage and told to behave, sat on Grandma's shoulder while Benson sat at her feet. I took a leaf out of Belinda's book and addressed the audience.

'I am going to sing a song, not currently in the charts. When you hear it you'll realize why. Those music lovers amongst you, or those of a nervous disposition, please feel free to leave the room now.'

Of course nobody did. They all wondered what was coming.

'Ten Green Bottles', that's what was coming.

By the time I had got down to seven green bottles, the audience were doubled up. I sang badly as usual. I didn't have to try, it just came naturally. Grandma seemed to be trying to keep me in tune by playing louder and louder and singing in the proper key. This only made me worse – as we had rehearsed. Benson crawled under the table and howled as only he can, and Mortimer squawked, 'Give us a break. Give us a break.'

This time we didn't give him a hard time.

We were a great hit. Mr Doig shook his head and wiped his eyes. The Drama teacher asked me later if I'd like to join the school Drama club next year, but the Music teacher didn't speak to me. I can't think why.

Grandma thought we had all done very well and treated us to some chips on the way home. I thought we had done well too and crossed my fingers and eyes when I went to look at the school noticeboard next day. The list of those who had got through the audition was up. About half of those who had entered made it through, including Belinda and the Beelines and the soon-to-be-world-famous, yours truly, Abigail Montgomery.

'Well done, Abby,' said Andy and Velvet. 'Great stuff.'

'Well done?' sniffed Belinda, who had spied

my name too. 'Not only do you look like a scarecrow but you sound like one too.'

'That's as may be,' said Andy, 'but she's the nicest scarecrow I know.'

Oh.

Well done, Andy.

I think.

It must be my ever-expanding, possibly super fit brain cells working overtime, but I've been thinking a lot about life recently. Have you ever noticed how, for a while, nothing much seems to happen. Life goes on at a steady rate, pretty boring sometimes, then, all of a sudden, WHAM, life-changing events come at you from all angles, pushing you this way and that till you're no longer sure which way is up. To say nothing of the hormones which suddenly wake up about now and think, Hey, time to create a little bit of havoc!

One minute I'm all grown-up, discussing the ways of the world with Mum or Grandma or Velvet. The next minute I'm in a panic because I can't find my old teddy. When this happens, he's usually in the wash because Mum has decided he's a hazard to health. Definitely hygienically challenged. But then so's Benson and she doesn't stick him in the washing machine at forty degrees. I can't bear to look at Ted's little face as he whizzes around on the spin cycle. I'm sure he hates it. I'm sure it jumbles up HIS brain cells. And I get really cross when Mum pegs him out by the ears to dry. I'm sure that can't be good for him. I would report her to the Society for the Protection of Teddy Bears, if there was one. Perhaps I should start one up. Hmm. Memo to self. Think about starting the SPTB.

But I digress. I was telling you about life, wasn't I? Well, it's looking up, especially for Mum. She came in the other day wearing a face-splitting grin. An ear to ear smile that said, 'Ask me why I'm so happy.' So I did.

'Why are you so happy?' I said. 'What's happened?'

'Guess,' she said.

I hate it when someone says that. I never get it right.

'A long-lost uncle has left you a strange gold necklace which has a curse on it, so you've sold the necklace for a fortune, and you're going to give me half of the lolly.'

'Nope.'

'Pity. Hmm. You've discovered 3 Pelham Way is sitting on top of an oilfield and we're moving to a castle in the meantime, till the millions roll in.'

'Close,' said Mum.

'Really?'

Mum gave me a withering look.

'Well, I don't know,' I said. I was getting fed up

with this game. 'Grandma's just told you that you and another baby were switched at birth and you're really a princess ... I don't know,' I said again. 'What's happened?'

'I finally got my partnership in the firm,' beamed Mum.

'Brilliant.' I threw my arms round her neck and hugged her. 'That's much better than being a princess with an oil well and a dodgy uncle.'

'Who's got a dodgy uncle?' asked Grandma, coming in with Benson from her afternoon dog walk.

'No one,' I grinned. 'Mum's just been made a partner in the firm.'

'Clever girl, you deserve it,' beamed Grandma and took Mum's hands and danced her round the room.

Benson and I joined in. Benson barking and me doing a few whoop-de-whoops not to be outdone. Handsome hurried in from the garden to find out what all the noise was about. His feet were muddy and his hands were oily, but Mum was in too good a mood to notice, even when he kissed her and left an oily smudge on her white shirt.

'This calls for a celebration,' said Grandma. 'Look in the cupboard, Abby, and break out the champagne.'

I looked in the cupboard, but it was in the same state as Old Mother Hubbard's.

'Er, will tea do instead?'

'I think David's coming round with some champagne,' blushed Mum.

'Oh, so David knows already. He knew before us.'

Why was I so annoyed? These hormones again probably.

'I phoned him,' said Mum. 'But I wanted to tell you face to face.'

Well, that's all right then.

David arrived at the front door before the kettle had boiled and it was champagne all round. I had a tiny taste, but the bubbles went right up my nose and made me sneeze, so I settled for Coke. No one wanted tea. David had also brought Mum a huge bouquet of red roses and was taking her out to dinner to celebrate. It was probably my hormones again, but I felt just a bit left out. After all, I'd been the one to put up with Mum all these years when she'd been studying. My thoughts must have shown in my face, because Grandma said, 'What's up, Abby? You've got a face like a week of wet Wednesdays.'

A look passed between Mum and David.

'Tell you what,' said David. 'Why don't we all go out to celebrate? My treat.'

'That's a good idea. What do you think, Abby?'

'I'll go and get changed,' I grinned.

'No rush,' said Mum. 'Plenty of time to do your homework before we go.'

I just knew she would say that.

We went to a posh little restaurant, tucked up a side street. It had very white table covers and napkins so stiff they kept sliding off our laps. I spent half my time under the table retrieving mine. I felt a bit like Benson: 'Here, Abby. Napkin, fetch!' There was a silver platter at each place and I thought WOW, if they fill these with food, that'll be ace!

No chance. Our food came on much smaller plates that sat inside the platters. The food was very carefully placed on the plates. A bit like the still-life arrangements Mad Max gets us to draw. But there was very little of it. Three bites and it was gone. Mum and David were too busy making eyes at each other to notice. During one of my forays under the table, I noticed that they were holding hands. Maybe we should have let them celebrate on their own.

Grandma obviously thought so too.

'It's getting late,' she said, 'and Abby has school tomorrow, so why don't we three go home now, Eva, and leave you and David to finish your coffee. We'll see you later.'

Mum agreed, and Handsome, Grandma and I slipped away.

'Strewth,' said Grandma, when we were outside, and out of earshot. 'Call that a meal? I've seen more meat on a butcher's apron. You two must still be starving.'

Handsome and I looked at each other and nodded.

'Me too,' said Grandma. 'Come on, race you to the chippy. Last one there's a baboon's backside.'

That's my Grandma.

# 19

After her good news, Mum was more cheerful. She didn't work any less hard, but she was much happier about it. The happiness spread like warm honey and the four of us and the pets were getting along quite nicely.

Till I saw the stranger. He was standing across the road looking at our house one day when I came home from school. I thought nothing of it at first. Lots of people stop and look at our house – mostly in amazement. It's the only one that has a large notice on the gate advertising Pets' Problems and luminous dinosaur footprints on the front lawn. Sometimes the ducks waddle round to the front too and people stop to feed them. They must be the fattest ducks in town by now. I don't know if they could fly away, even if they wanted to. So someone looking at the house was hardly new, though I'd never seen anyone with a baseball cap and such an enormous black beard there before. Then I saw him the next day and the next.

I started to worry. Could he be from the Australian mafia? Had they finally caught up with Handsome? Mum had gone through all Handsome's documents from the sale of the sheep farm in Oz, and the money he had paid to the Revenue in back taxes. All that was in order. It was the money he had borrowed from the Ozzie mafia and had paid back that there were no receipts for that was the problem.

'You were desperate and daft, but not dishonest, Handsome,' Mum told him. 'Crooks don't like receipts. They don't like anything that can be traced.'

'I thought I could just pay them back what I owed and that would be an end to it,' said Handsome. 'I didn't realize they would keep coming back for more and more money.' But Mum was convinced Handsome was now quite safe.

'They won't want to stir up trouble in this country over such a small amount that you've more than paid back anyway,' she said.

We had all relaxed because Mum is so sensible and positive about these kind of things.

But now, there was this strange man. He was only there when I came home from school. I didn't see him at any other times because I peeked out of my bedroom window to check. Rosie liked to sit on the window ledge and watch the world go by.

'Who do you think he could be, Rosie?' I whispered. 'Do you think he's part of the Australian mafia? Do you think Handsome's in trouble? I don't want to tell Mum because she's been so happy recently. What should I do?'

Rosie leapt on to my shoulder, her sharp little claws digging into my school sweater.

'You think I should tell Grandma and Handsome?'

Rosie licked my ear.

'Yes, I think so too.'

Fortunately, Mum went out to the gym that night. Spring was coming and she had just tried on her favourite pale blue jeans. No chance. The zip came halfway up, gave up and slid back down again.

'These must have shrunk in the wash,' Mum muttered.

'Uhuh,' grinned Grandma, 'or you've spread a bit.'

'I like a bit of fat on a woman,' said Handsome, trying to be helpful.

Mum glared at the pair of them and went in search of her sports bag. As soon as I heard her drive off I told Grandma and Handsome about the man.

'You say he's only there when you come home from school, Abby,' frowned Grandma.

I nodded.

'That's when I'm out with the dogs.'

'And I'm either out in the truck or working in the back garden,' said Handsome. 'So there's no one else in the house then.'

'It's probably nothing,' said Grandma. 'Let's not meet trouble halfway. But, tomorrow I'll walk the dogs early and Handsome will stay home so we can see what happens. We'll keep an eye out from behind the curtains in your bedroom, Abby. Don't worry about it. We'll sort it out. You were right not to mention it to your mum. No point in upsetting her if it's nothing.'

Lessons dragged next day in school. I couldn't concentrate on anything very much for thinking about the strange man. I know Grandma said not to worry, but my over-fertile imagination wouldn't let it go. Supposing there was more than one strange man. Supposing there was a whole gang of them disguised as postmen, road menders, telephone engineers, etc. I'd seen a movie once where that had happened. Supposing they had come to kidnap Handsome and take him back to Oz. Supposing they decided to take me instead. I'm only half his size and weight, although I eat as much. They could hold me to ransom till Handsome paid them back what they said he owed. Or, supposing the man in the baseball cap and big black beard was really an alien in disguise. I told you I'm sure they're out there.

'Abigail Montgomery,' said Mr Soames, my Maths teacher, 'if it wouldn't inconvenience you too much perhaps you'd like to try the odd little bit of geometry today. Nothing too taxing, you understand. Maybe just draw a triangle, or a circle. Possibly a parallelogram, if that's not too hard. You know, just to please me. So I can go home a happy teacher knowing I've taught you something today. Justified my existence, so to speak.'

'Pardon?' I said. I hadn't even been listening properly.

'Just get on with your work,' Mr Soames said sadly. He gets really down if his little witticisms are wasted.

I told Andy and Velvet all about Blackbeard, as I now called the stranger, and they wanted to come home with me for protection.

'No, it's all right,' I laughed. 'Grandma and Handsome will be watching and they're all the protection I need.'

And they were. Blackbeard did nothing more than look over at the house as I came back from school, then he disappeared off down the road.

Grandma and Handsome were puzzled. What was Blackbeard up to?

'Trouble is he's not doing anything,' said Grandma. 'Just looking at the house. There's no law against that.'

'It's not like you to worry about the law, Aphrodite,' grinned Handsome.

'It's living with Eva that does it,' said Grandma.

'She's so law-abiding, it eventually rubs off. But we must do something.'

'Perhaps we could get the pensioners to keep a lookout,' I said. 'They're around most of the day.'

'Good idea,' said Grandma, and immediately phoned round and alerted her friends. From then on not a mouse moved, not a snail sneezed, not a beetle blinked in Pelham Way, but somebody knew about it.

'Right,' said Grandma, when Blackbeard had been there every day for nearly a week. 'Time for some action.'

She called a meeting of the pensioners one afternoon just after Blackbeard had gone.

'Tomorrow we nab him,' she told them.

'I'll be in the street with my walking stick,' said Mrs Polanski. 'I'll trip him up if he causes trouble.'

'I could ask him the time to distract him while you come out of the house,' volunteered shy Miss Flack. 'I always fancied being a spy.'

'And I'll wrestle him to the ground, if needs be,' said Major Knotts, 'with Handsome's help, of course.'

I could hardly wait. Talk about excitement. 'What shall I do?' I asked.

'Watch from the window,' said Grandma.

'Just watch?' I squeaked.

'Yes,' said Handsome, 'and no arguments.'

I put my hands on my hips and gave him my best glare. And, do you know what, he gave me an even better one right back. Then I remembered that for all Handsome seemed so gentle, he had wrestled crocodiles and won.

'I'll watch from the window,' I muttered.

Next day at school came and went. I went through it on automatic pilot, then hurried home. When I turned the corner into Pelham Way, Blackbeard was there. I saw a curtain twitch. So was Mrs Polanski. She came out of her house as I reached her gate.

'Hello, Abby,' she winked. 'I'll just walk with you a little.'

A less likely bodyguard would have been hard to imagine. But Mrs Polanski had a mean streak.

'I have a large Polish sausage in my bag,' she whispered, 'and if he cuts up rough, I'll let him have it on the nose. Otherwise, I'll have it for my tea.'

I couldn't help laughing.

Then, Major Knotts appeared in army camouflage gear, walking along the street apparently reading his paper. Miss Flack passed him without a word. Then she looked at her watch and gave it a little shake. A small frown creased her forehead and she crossed the road to ask Blackbeard if he knew the time. She was fantastic. That woman should be on the stage or in the Secret Service. By this time, my 'escort' had left me at my front gate. I ran inside.

Grandma and Handsome passed me in the hall.

'Upstairs window,' Handsome ordered as he left through the front door.

I flew upstairs, anxious to miss nothing.

I pressed my nose up against the glass. What WAS happening? Grandma and Handsome were speaking to Blackbeard. What were they saying? I saw Grandma throw up her hands and Handsome shake his head. Who was Blackbeard really?

He didn't look like the Australian mafia – no champagne corks hanging from his baseball cap. And there'd been nothing in the news recently about a mad axe murderer. Anyway, there was no axe to be seen. I bit my fingernails in frustration. Then Grandma and Handsome started back across the road. *Bringing the man with them.*

Oh boy!

## 20

The man didn't look too frightening. Grandma practically marched him into the sitting room.

I watched in amazement as he took off his baseball cap and his beard came with it.

Underneath, his face was vaguely familiar. I looked at him closely. He looked at me closely.

'This man,' said Grandma, 'who has given us so much worry this week, Abby, this man, I am sorry to have to tell you, is your father.'

'My dad,' I whispered. And I must have sounded really shocked because Rosie immediately jumped up into my arms and Benson came and leaned his supportive weight against my leg.

'Hello, Abby,' said my dad.

For once, I was lost for words. What do you say to a dad who disappears before you were born then turns up thirteen years later wearing a false beard?

Mortimer knew. '/##'#''#***,' he said.

For once, nobody gave him a hard time.

We were all just standing there when the front door banged open and Mum was home.

'Hulloooo,' she called, and opened the sitting-room door. She took one look at my dad, turned white, and sank gracefully to the floor in a dead faint.

That broke the silence. Everyone rushed to help. Handsome picked Mum up like she was a rag doll and gently sat her in a chair. Grandma put Mum's head between her knees. Undignified, but effective. Mum came to with Benson running round and round her chair barking anxiously. Meantime, Rosie, not to be outdone, had spied the black beard on the coffee table and decided to stalk it.

Mum looked very pale, her eyes large and luminous in her head.

'I'll get some water,' I said.

'I'll help you,' said my dad.

I really didn't need any help to fetch a glass of water, but I let him come into the kitchen anyway. It felt really odd having this strange man, who was my dad, in our kitchen. Suddenly the kitchen felt weird, not like our kitchen at all, but like . . . like a stage set where the people aren't real people, but actors acting out their parts.

'Where are the glasses kept?' asked my dad.

'Top shelf,' I said, pointing to a cupboard.

He got down a glass and held it under the tap while I turned on the water. We looked at each other. Brown eyes looking into brown eyes, drinking in what we saw. The water overflowed the glass, ran down his hand and soaked his sleeve.

'Sorry,' I said.

'S'OK.'

I dried the glass on a tea towel and took the water to Mum. She was sitting bolt upright in the chair, still pale, but otherwise fine. You could easily tell she was better by the icy tone she directed at my dad.

'What are you doing here?' she asked.

'I wanted to see my daughter.'

'You left it a bit late.'

'Thirteen years,' I whispered.

'I've always regretted walking out,' said my dad quietly. 'You may not believe that, but it's true. Thirteen years ago I just wasn't grown-up enough to cope with a baby.'

'And I was,' muttered Mum.

'You always were.'

'What do you want?'

'To get to know Abby, and make up for lost time, if that's possible. I know I don't deserve it, but that's what I'd like to do.'

Mum looked at him for a long moment. Was she seeing the young man she fell in love with all these years ago? I looked at him and saw a tall, rather gangly man with crinkly auburn hair. He was my dad all right, but he was a stranger.

'I think Abby will need time to think this over. Time to decide whether she wants to see you or not,' said Mum. 'It's been a shock for all of us. Leave your address and phone number and someone will be in touch.'

My dad opened his mouth to say something, then decided against it.

'Fine,' he said. He handed me a card with his address and phone number on it, gave me a little smile and left.

The four of us stood and looked at each other. There was an awkward silence in the room as everyone thought their own thoughts. Inside my head it felt like my brain cells were buzzing and excited. All chattering away at once, sending messages to each other, trying to make sense of what had just happened. Judging by the looks on the faces of the others, they felt exactly the same.

'Well,' said Grandma, first to recover. 'I think we all need a cup of tea. Hot and sweet is good for shock.'

'Good idea,' said Handsome, and followed her into the kitchen.

Mum gave me an anxious look.

'Are you all right, Abby? Do you want to sit down?'

I nodded and went and sat on the floor beside her chair. Mum ran her fingers through my crinkly hair.

'Well,' she said. 'You haven't said anything. What do you think?'

'I don't know,' I mumbled. 'I'll have to think about things. It's too much to decide . . . I don't know. He looks like me . . .'

'Especially without the baseball cap and the false beard,' said Grandma, appearing with a tray of mugs.

'What?' asked Mum, and we filled her in on the details of the past week.

'You should have told me,' was all she said, and she suddenly looked rather sad.

I drank my tea. Benson sat down beside me, partly for comfort, but mostly to scrounge some of my chocolate biscuit.

'Where's Rosie?' I asked. 'She usually likes to lick my fingers when I've been eating chocolate.'

I looked round and spotted her. She was on the coffee table, fast asleep inside the baseball cap. She was obviously tired after her battle with the false beard. It lay beside her, shredded into bits.

## 21

I didn't sleep much that night. I don't think Mum did either. She looked as bleary-eyed as I did next morning.

We'd had a long talk the night before, and she'd made it perfectly plain it was entirely up to me whether or not I wanted to have contact with my dad.

'You won't upset me either way, Abby,' she said. 'So take your time and decide what *you* really want.'

Trouble was, after thinking about it all night, I still didn't know.

'You can stay off school today if you like,' said Mum over breakfast. 'If you need some more time to get over the shock of meeting your dad.'

Stay off school! Mum really was concerned about me. I usually had to prove I had the plague and was infectious at a hundred paces before that happened.

I smiled at her.

'Are you staying off work?'

'No.'

'Then I'm going to school.'

'That's my girl.' She winked and gave me a quick hug. 'See you tonight.' And she disappeared in a cloud of perfume. She always gives herself an extra squirt when she's feeling upset.

Grandma and Benson came in from their walk. Benson gave me a paw in the hope I'd give him a bit of toast. Grandma gave me a searching look.

'The red-eyed look's in fashion this week,' I told her.

'And you're always in fashion,' she smiled. 'Handsome and I thought we might pick you up from school today and take you for a slap-up tea somewhere. Somewhere where the portions aren't for anorexic ants.'

'Sounds good to me,' I said, and gave Benson the last buttery bit of crust. 'But what about the afternoon dog walk?'

'Miss Flack and Major Knotts will do it for me.'

Wrinklies to the rescue once more.

I went off to school, my head full of mixed-up thoughts. None of them about school work. I waited till lunchtime, till we were all together, before telling Andy and Velvet what had happened. Then I swore them to secrecy.

'Are you all right?' they wanted to know.

'Everybody's been asking me that, but I'm fine. It was a bit of a shock, that's all, but I'm fine.'

I think I thought if I kept saying that, it might be true. I might convince myself.

'What are you going to do?' asked Andy.

'I don't know,' I said. 'I'm all muddled up. For years I've wondered what my dad was like, but now I've met him, and have the chance to get to know him, I just don't know. I don't know if knowing him would be better than not knowing him.'

Velvet gave my arm a squeeze.

'You need time, Abby,' she said. 'Don't rush at it. You need time to adjust to the idea that your dad is there for you, if you want him.'

That's Velvet. Sensible as always.

'You're right,' I said. 'I'll let it be and see what happens. See how I feel.'

And I tried to think about other things.

But the problem of my dad was out there now, and I knew that sooner or later I'd have to come to a decision. But it didn't have to be today. I didn't have to decide immediately if I wanted to get to know my dad. After all, it had taken him thirteen years to decide he wanted to get to know me.

# 22

I have another theory. This one is Abigail Montgomery's Theory of Coincidence, i.e. is it a coincidence that when one thing comes along and turns your life upside-down, another is waiting just behind to have its turn?

I had no sooner got over the shock of seeing my dad when my mum came up with another one.

'David and I are getting married,' she announced one night over the vegetable chilli.

I choked on a kidney bean. Handsome thumped me on the back and the bean shot out of my throat and landed on the floor. Benson and Rosie immediately played football with it.

'Good,' Grandma said to Mum. 'I'm delighted to hear it.'

'Congratulations,' beamed Handsome. 'I like David. He's a nice fellow.'

'Married?' I said, my voice sounding strange to my own ears. 'Married?'

I liked David too, but Mum and David married?

'Married, married,' squawked Mortimer.

'Shut up, Mortimer,' said everyone.

Mortimer looked hurt. What was rude about saying 'Married'?

'But David's just your boyfriend,' I burst out. 'Grandma and I just organized Operation Boyfriend to get you out and about a bit more, so you could have some fun. We didn't organize Operation Wedding.'

'Well, it's your own fault,' said Mum. 'Operation Boyfriend was so successful that now it's Operation Wedding. I hope you're pleased.'

Pleased? I wasn't sure about that.

'Are you going to tell us your other news too, Eva?' Grandma asked, smiling.

Mum blushed. 'What other news?' she said.

'I think you know,' said Grandma.

'I can't keep anything from you,' said Mum. 'You know me too well.'

'I'm your mother,' said Grandma.

'Look,' I said. 'Maybe I'm just thick, but I seem to be missing something here. Did I black out? Have I gone deaf? Was there a time slip? What are you on about?'

'I'm in the dark too,' said Handsome.

Mum looked at us all and took a deep breath.

'I'm going to have a baby,' she said.

WHAAAAAAAT!!!!

'That's wonderful,' said Grandma and hugged Mum.

'Beaut,' grinned Handsome. 'I like babies.'

They all looked at me. I was just sitting there, stunned, fork halfway to my mouth, vegetable chilli congealing on my school tie.

'Well, what do you think, Abby?' said Mum.

What did I think? *What did I think?* All of a sudden everyone wanted to know what I thought. Is this what growing up is all about? All this thinking?

'I think adults are inconsistent,' I said, using one of my favourite big words.

'Inconsistent?' Mum looked puzzled.

'How many times have you warned me not to get pregnant?'

Mum had the good grace to look sheepish.

'I know, but this is different.'

'Not another immaculate conception surely,' I sniffed. I'd been listening when we'd done comparative religions in school.

Grandma snorted. Handsome grinned.

Mum wriggled a bit. 'No, but . . .'

'Stop giving your mother a hard time, Abby,' said Grandma. 'No one's perfect. Not your mum, not you, not any of us.'

Perfect? I don't think I'm perfect. Belinda Fishcake thinks she's perfect, and I'm not like her. Am I? A horrible vision of me dressed in pink, complete with pink bows in my hair, swam in front of my eyes.

'I'm not wearing a frilly pink frock to the wedding,' I said illogically.

Relieved, Mum laughed. 'Not even as the only bridesmaid?'

'Bridesmaid? You want me to be your bridesmaid?'

'Of course,' said Mum. 'If you've got over the shock, we have a lot to talk about.'

'This sounds like women's work,' said Handsome. 'I don't know a lot about frocks, so I'll just go out to the shed and check on the animals.' And he went off whistling.

The three of us faced each other.

'A wedding,' I said.

'A baby,' said Grandma.

'A husband,' said Mum. 'And a whole new way of life. What have you two done to me?'

'We sorted you out,' smiled Grandma, 'and now we'll sort out the consequences.'

Oh boy!

# 23

David and Mum had already agreed that it should just be a quiet family wedding.

'We don't want any fuss,' said Mum. 'David's going to wear his kilt – the Anderson tartan's very nice – and Peter and Prof Charlie will wear kilts as well. So I thought if our outfits could co-ordinate too . . .'

No fuss. Yeah right. Some hope. I thought maybe no fuss meant I could turn up in my best jeans or maybe my last disco outfit. Grandma obviously thought the same.

'I can't wear Old Belle then,' she said.

'No pets,' said Mum tartly.

'That means Benson and Rosie and Mortimer are banned too,' I said.

'This is a wedding,' Mum told me, 'not an outing to the zoo.'

The discussion/argument went on. The wedding reception was to be in a small local hotel. Mum had already tried on a dress that she liked, but the wedding would have to be soon while she still fitted into it.

'It's pale buttermilk yellow with pink gossamer floaty bits,' she said dreamily. 'Totally delicious.'

'Do you wear it or eat it?' I muttered. I was definitely not going to be dressed up like an ice-cream sundae, not even for Mum.

'And it has a tiny matching hat,' went on Mum, ignoring me completely.

'A hat,' I yelped. This was getting worse and worse. 'I hope you're not expecting me to wear a hat. Someone might see me.'

'The three of us will go shopping on Saturday,' said Mum, 'and see what we can find.'

What a recipe for disaster.

Usually Saturdays can't come quickly enough for me, but I was dreading this one.

'I'll probably need at least two pizzas on Saturday afternoon to recover,' I said when I told Andy all the news the next day. 'Mum and I can never agree about what I should wear.'

But Grandma had a word with me before we set off the following Saturday morning.

'This wedding is your mum's big day, Abby,' she said. 'So it's really up to her what she'd like us to wear. We'd best try to agree if we can.'

Tall order.

We went to a very fancy salon that sold wedding outfits. The shop was so posh I nearly wiped my feet before I went in. Mum had already been in and seen what she wanted Grandma to wear. It was a soft pink silk suit with matching shoes. That was bad enough, but she thought I'd look lovely in a yellow sticky-out frock with flounces. I opened my mouth to ask if the frock belonged to one of Cinderella's Ugly Sisters, but Grandma gave me a look and I shut it again.

We tried on the outfits. Grandma first. She was in the changing room for ages, muttering. Then she came out. What a surprise. She looked really good in the suit. The soft pink went well with her rosy cheeks, but the pink shoes did not look so good with the stripy knee-high socks she'd worn under her jeans.

'I think Madam may want to rethink her hosiery for the wedding,' said the snooty sales assistant.

'Hosiery?' I muttered to Mum.

'Socks and tights and things,' Mum muttered back.

I tried on the Ugly Sister frock. It was even worse than I thought. The flounces showed off my knobbly knees and my elbows stuck out from beneath the puff sleeves.

I slouched out of the changing room and stood in front of Mum.

'Stand up straight, Abby,' she said.

'I am standing up straight,' I said, and stood up straight.

The flounces moved from my knees to halfway up my thighs.

Mum frowned. 'I don't think it's quite you,' she said.

Five shops and several arguments later we still hadn't found anything that was quite me. The dresses either made me look like Abby in Wonderland or . . .

'A tart,' said Grandma frankly.

There seemed to be nothing in between. Finally I escaped the Frocky Horror Show and went to meet Andy.

'Well,' he grinned, 'was it a two-pizza morning?'

'Two pizzas and a large ice-cream,' I said.

'As bad as that? What are you going to do? You can't be a bridesmaid in your school uniform.'

'I'll speak to Miss Flack,' I said. 'She's my only hope.'

# 24

Miss Flack came to the rescue, as she so often has in the past.

Mum and I went round to see her in her little house across the field. I love her house. It's full of cushions and curtains and tapestries she's made herself. Thomas, the kitten Miss Flack had got from Grandma, was sitting inside Miss Flack's bag of embroidery wools when we went in. He had obviously settled in well.

'How nice to see you both,' said Miss Flack. 'Do come in and sit down. I hear you have lots of good news.'

We didn't have to tell her about the wedding or the baby then.

'News travels fast in these parts,' she smiled.

'Have you heard we can't find a frock for me to wear to the wedding that doesn't make me look like something the cat's dragged in? No offence, Thomas.'

Thomas hopped out of the wool bag and

came over to investigate my trainers.

'I did,' laughed Miss Flack, 'and I've been expecting you. Aphrodite told me about your colour scheme and I went out and picked up a few small samples of material that might be suitable. Do you see anything you like, Abby?'

Now why couldn't Mum take a sensible approach like that?

There was something I liked. A tiny piece of material the colour of a sunny cornfield.

'Good choice,' said Miss Flack, 'and perfect with your hair colour.'

Even Mum agreed.

'But what style of frock?' she said. 'Abby's so difficult to please.'

Moi? Difficult?

'Well,' said Miss Flack, 'I think either an elegant, ankle-length shift dress or narrow trousers and a tunic or coat top would be good. A young style and not too formal.'

In the end we settled on trousers and a tunic top, and I went home happy. I no longer worried about how the clothes would turn out. Miss Flack was a genius. She was one of my best friends beside Andy and Velvet. Funny how friends don't have to be the same age, isn't it? Ever since she'd made me my first outfit for the school disco she and I had been friends. Sometimes I'd go with Grandma to visit her, sometimes I'd go on my own. She has no family of her own and was always pleased to see me.

'You are so lucky to have a family,' she'd said to me more than once.

I agreed with her, though there were times when certain members of my family could be a real pain in the neck.

But who'd have thought Mum would have got married again? Who'd have thought she'd have another baby? Funny how you think you know someone, especially someone like your mum whom you see every day, and then you find out you don't really know them at all. Trouble is you only see your mum as your mum, not as a separate person. Uh-oh, I can feel another one of my theories coming on. I'm becoming so intelligent these days it's really quite worrying.

There was something else worrying me too. I hadn't mentioned it to Mum because there had been so much happening recently with my dad turning up, the wedding, the new baby, etc., I didn't want to add to the problems, but the worry was there and it wouldn't go away. So, having solved the problem of my wedding outfit, I spoke to Mum about it on the way back from Miss Flack's.

'You know how we've got lots of family now?'

'Uhuh.'

'You know how you're going to marry David and he has a son?'

'Uhuh.'

'You know how you're going to have a baby?'

'Uhuh.'

Mum knew a lot, but did she know the answer to this next question?

'Where are we all going to live?'

There, it was out, I'd said it. Mum always complains about how small our house is now that Grandma and Handsome and the pets are living with us. How were we going to fit in all the others?

Mum looked thoughtful.

'I was waiting for you to ask that,' she said. 'So I thought, since Peter only stays with his dad at weekends, he could have the sofa, and you could move out into the Pets' Problems shed and let the new baby have your room . . .'

'*Whaaaaat?*'

'I'm joking,' said Mum. 'Obviously we'll have to find somewhere bigger to live. David has a friend who wants to buy his flat and I'll have to sell our house.'

'But where will we go?' I asked. Suddenly my little untidy bedroom at 3 Pelham Way was very important to me. Suddenly it was my only refuge from the storm. Suddenly I could see myself cast out in the cold, cold snow with nowhere to go. Trudging along the road in my school uniform which had inexplicably become tattered and torn, carrying my only possessions in a bundle on a stick.

I shook my head to clear the impression from my mind. Sometimes a fertile imagination can be a very uncomfortable thing.

'I don't know where we'll go just yet,' said Mum. 'Hopefully not too far away from all our friends. David and I have been looking for a suitable place for some time, but we might just have to squash up for a while till something turns up.'

'But I don't need to move out into the Pets' Problems shed?'

'That really was a joke,' said Mum. 'The animals will have to stay in there. No, it's the Quiet House for you, I'm afraid. Think of how much homework you'll get done in the peace and quiet, and I'm sure you can learn to sleep sitting up.'

Sometimes my mother thinks she is so funny!

# 25

Meantime, in the middle of all this there was still school, and homework and other minor inconveniences.

Somehow news of Mum's pregnancy and forthcoming wedding had reached Cosgrove High. Word had spread so quickly you'd have thought Mr Doig had announced it at assembly. Even Mrs Jackson came up to me in the corridor and asked me how Mum was keeping.

'She's fine, she's not been ill,' I said, before I realized what she meant.

'She's fine,' I repeated.

'Tell her I still have a cot up in my attic, if she wants to borrow it. No point in buying a new one unless she's going to have several more babies.'

Several more babies. I hadn't thought of that. Help!

Then I had another shock in History class. Usually I just sit and gaze at Mr Morrison because he's so yummy, then I blush when he asks me a question because I haven't a clue what he's been saying. But today he asked me to stay behind after class for a moment.

Velvet raised her eyebrows at me. 'What have you done?' the eyebrows said.

I shrugged my shoulders. 'Search me,' the shoulders replied.

I stayed behind. Mr Morrison gave me that lovely crinkly-eyed smile he has and asked, 'How's your mum?'

'She's fine, thank you.'

Here we go again, I thought. Maybe I should pin up a health report on the school noticeboard.

TO WHOM IT MAY CONCERN
Eva Montgomery is fine. Apart from one minor fainting fit under very difficult circumstances. She has not been sick, nauseous or had any cravings for gherkins, pickled onions or coal. At least, no more than normal.

Signed,
Abigail Montgomery
(Head Nurse)

But if I did that someone would be sure to alter the last bit to Head Case, so I wouldn't risk it.

Mr Morrison was chatting while he gathered up his books.

'Your mum and I were at university together, you know,' he said.

No, I didn't know.

'Different courses, naturally. But we saw each other at student discos occasionally. Very bright girl.'

Girl?!?!

'Give her my regards. Tell her Johnnie Morrison says, "Hi".'

I nodded dumbly. My favourite teacher and my mum knew each other. Had possibly danced together. Had possibly FANCIED each other.

'******###!!' as Mortimer would say.

In deep shock, I went off in search of Velvet to tell her what had happened, but before I could find her Belinda and the Beelines found me.

'I hear you're going to be a big sister,' said Belinda.

'Uhuh.'

'Well, I'm keeping my fingers crossed the baby will be all right.'

'Thank you,' I said, and thought, She's being really nice. Maybe I've misjudged her.

'I'm keeping my fingers crossed the baby will be normal and not look like you. Who'd want a scarecrow baby? Who could love a scarecrow baby?' she sneered.

The Beelines laughed uproariously, and Belinda smirked. It was the smirk that did it. I looked at it, exploded, and smacked her one. Right across it. And, for two seconds, it felt right. It felt good, till the Beelines jumped on me and defended their precious Belinda.

I'd never been at the bottom of a rugby scrum before. Fortunately the bell for the next class saved me from too much damage, though I was too angry to feel much pain, and tried to give as good as I got. The mauling, I was sure, had left me looking even more like a scarecrow than normal. But a scarecrow baby! No one was going to call my little brother/sister that and get away with it.

In Art, if Mad Max noticed that my nose was bleeding and I was even scruffier than normal he didn't say. But he did say my painting of a stormy sky was really good. That I'd got a lot of feeling, a lot of passion into it.

'Thank you,' I smiled at him painfully through a swollen lip. But I didn't tell him I'd pretended it was Fishcake's face I was sloshing the paint on.

I wonder if that's the secret of good painting?

I wonder why I'd defended a tiny unborn baby like I had?

I wonder if life will ever be normal again?

Answers in your best writing, in green ink, in triplicate, by tomorrow, please.

# 26

Dental appointment after school today. I was not looking forward to it. More torture, probably, as Mr Douglas tightens up the screw on my braces. He always does it with a smile too. A perfect smile. Why is it dentists have all got nice straight teeth? Is that a requirement for dental school? Do you have to have so many A-levels and a good set of gnashers before they let you in? Do dentists ever forget to clean their teeth? Do they ever eat sweets? Do they ever have (whisper it) false teeth? I would ask Mr Douglas, but it's really difficult asking intelligent questions with rubber-gloved fingers down your throat.

But it didn't matter, because all the questions went out of my head when Mr Douglas said the magic words . . .

'Your brace can come off today.'

'What?' I nearly leapt out of the chair.

'Your brace can come off today.'

Perhaps that's why he always says everything

twice, because nobody believes him the first time.

'Fantastic,' I said, and could say no more as he carefully removed the train tracks, cleaned off the dental cement and handed me a mirror.

'Have a look. Have a look.'

I didn't need to be told twice.

Wow! Straight teeth. No longer goofy or rabbity, but straight up and down. I can now smile without frightening animals and small children. And just in time for the wedding.

I could have kissed Mr Douglas, except I didn't. Instead, I just burbled on about the wedding and how it would be great to look normal for the photographs.

Mr Douglas smiled. 'You're the bridesmaid. You must look good.'

I agreed and it was only when I was halfway downstairs that I wondered if absolutely everybody in the town knew about the wedding.

When I got home, Miss Flack had delivered my wedding outfit. It's brilliant. Miss Flack had lined the tunic in the same soft pink as Grandma's suit and little flashes of it showed where the tunic split at the sides. She'd sewed little pink roses on to the covered buttons down the front and they match the roses Mum is going to have in her bouquet.

I'm getting quite excited about this wedding now. It won't be long, only a few more days. Mum and David are going away on honeymoon for a week and Grandma is left in charge. Should be fun. Grandma has got her 'hosiery' sorted out. Totally uninteresting flesh-coloured tights, but they do look better with the pink shoes than the socks did. Try as she might, Mum couldn't get her to agree to wear a hat, and I said a very definite NO WAY to flowers in my hair, but Mum's going to wear a single rose in hers. That's all right. She's the bride. She doesn't have to worry about her street cred.

Handsome, not to be outdone, has bought himself a Harris tweed jacket. He looks good in it. He scrubs up quite well.

Mum is getting so nervous about the wedding. So is David. If he's not round here seeing Mum, he's on the phone. I'm beginning to get used to him being about the place. I really like him, so that helps, but it's not like he was a proper dad, always there from the start. I'll never have that. I'll never know what that's like.

I still haven't phoned my real dad. Perhaps he thinks I've forgotten about him, but I haven't. It's just that there's been so much happening lately, my mind's been in a bit of a jumble. When I start to think about my dad, I get sidetracked into thinking about David coming to stay here, then I get to thinking about the wedding, then where we'll all eventually live, then . . . I forget what I started off thinking about.

Can you have too much on your mind? Can

your mind expand to take in everything you want it to without bursting? Does it have elasticated side panels for really big thoughts? Or, can it go into overload and get tired and shut down like a dodgy computer?

One of my school reports stated that I had an enquiring mind, but Mum said that was teacher speak for, 'This girl never shuts up' or, more politely, 'This girl asks too many questions'. But I don't think you can ever do that. I don't think you can ever know enough. At the moment I'm having to learn a lot of things very fast. I feel like one of those plants on a nature programme where the camera has been speeded up so you can see the plant growing at a hundred times its normal rate. The stem shoots up, the buds appear and the leaves unfold before your eyes. It's an exciting feeling, but a bit strange, and sometimes I just want to slide back down into the warmth of the earth where it's safe. But I can't. Nobody can. Once you start growing up, there's no stopping it. I'll be a fully grown-up adult soon. What a scary thought. Where's my old teddy?

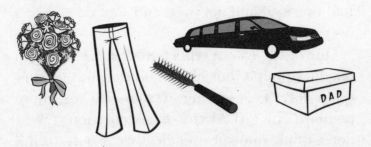

## 27

The day of the wedding dawned bright and clear. Grandma was up early and took Mum her breakfast in bed. I heard them chatting so I got up and went to join them. I'd forgotten to put on my dressing gown so I slid into bed beside Mum to keep cosy. I hadn't done that since I was six.

Mum gave me her toast.

'I don't think I can eat anything,' she said. 'I'm so nervous. Am I doing the right thing, turning our lives upside down? I haven't known David that long. Perhaps I should postpone the wedding for a while just to be sure. What do you think?'

Grandma smiled.

'I think you should try to eat some breakfast then have a leisurely bath and get yourself ready to be Mrs Anderson.'

Mrs Anderson. I hadn't thought of that.

'I don't have to change my name, do I?' I asked.

'No,' smiled Mum. 'I don't have to either, but I quite fancy being Mrs Anderson.'

'There you are then,' said Grandma. 'Now drink your tea and I'll make you some more toast. Your bridesmaid seems to have scoffed the last lot.'

Oops.

Mum took ages in the bathroom and used up most of the hot water, so the rest of us had very quick lukewarm showers. I spent a long time getting ready. At least ten minutes more than normal. I spent extra time cleaning my beautiful straight teeth, and extra time straightening my unruly hair. I may even have put on a smidgeon of eye shadow and a smudge of lip gloss. After all, it was a special occasion.

Mum was a beautiful bride. She looked like she was lit up from the inside. Grandma was a beautiful mother of the bride. She was just so happy to see Mum happy. And the bridesmaid, well, what can I say? She was stunning!

So Handsome said anyway.

A sleek black limo came for us at 11.30 a.m. and whisked us off to the marriage suite, in the centre of town. David was waiting there for Mum. One look at how he gazed at her when she got out of the car was enough to tell us she was doing the right thing. I don't think David saw anyone else but her. Certainly not me or Grandma. But Prof Charlie and Peter saw us. They looked splendid in their kilts and thought we looked pretty good too.

At least Prof Charlie did. Peter gave me a funny look.

'You look different today,' he said. 'More like a girl.'

I was going to make a smart remark about boys wearing skirts, but was glad I didn't when he went on . . . 'You look more like a sister today. I've never had a sister before.'

A sister! Of course. I had been so busy thinking about the changes to my life that I'd completely forgotten about the changes to Peter's.

'I've never had a brother before either,' I said. 'It'll be cool.'

'But not as cool as this kilt is when the wind blows,' he replied. We both giggled and went into the marriage suite together.

I don't know what I was expecting, but the wedding ceremony was all over in about twenty minutes. The registrar was a very smiley lady who explained all that would happen. I didn't really have to do anything except hold Mum's bouquet while she signed the register. But I did have a big lump in my throat when she looked at David and said, 'I do'. I looked to see if Peter felt the same when his dad said, 'I do', but he was busy scratching his knee at the time. I think his kilt probably itched.

After that it was outside for the photographs. I had to remember to smile nicely and not do my usual Dracula impression. Actually, that wasn't so effective now that my fangs had been straightened. Fortunately there weren't too many photographs taken because it was still early spring and a bit chilly. Grandma muttered she wished she had Old Belle around her.

Handsome was going to take off his new Harris tweed jacket to give to her but Grandma stopped him.

'I only ironed the bit of your shirt that shows,' she grinned.

The sleek black limo appeared again and whisked us off to the hotel where a small private room had been reserved for the wedding party.

'Just a quiet lunch,' said Mum. 'We didn't want any fuss.'

But, when we went in, there was a surprise. Grandma had organized Mrs Polanski, Miss Flack and Major Knotts to bring along the pets. So there, waiting for us, were Benson with a big blue bow on his collar, Rosie with a pink ribbon round hers, and Mortimer who'd been taught a new word.

'Congratulations. Congratulations,' he squawked.

Mum and David laughed. They were delighted with the surprise. They cut the pink and white wedding cake and the pets got a little bit each while we had some champagne. I quite liked the champagne this time. Does that mean I really am growing up?

We had a superb lunch, and, later on that day, Mum and David flew off to Paris for a week's honeymoon. It was strange going home in a taxi without Mum. I felt a bit flat after the earlier excitement of the wedding.

I changed out of my wedding outfit and into my old jeans. Grandma and Handsome did likewise. Grandma cooked us our favourite sausage, egg and chips for tea and gave Benson some too because he was wandering around a bit, missing Mum. Then Grandma disappeared upstairs and came back with a big brown envelope.

'Handsome and I have something to show you,' she said.

She took some sheets of paper out of the envelope and handed them to me. They contained details of a big old house.

'What do you think of that?' asked Grandma.

'Looks great. Apart from the bits that are falling down.'

'We can soon fix that,' said Handsome.

I looked at the pair of them. They were grinning like a couple of kids.

'You mean we could live there,' I said.

Grandma nodded. 'Handsome and I have been looking at possible houses too. Your mum wants us all to stay together, and we need to if she's going to go back to work after the baby's born.'

'So, we need somewhere big enough . . .'

'For all of us, for Pets' Problems and Handsome's business. This house would be ideal once it's fixed up.'

'So?'

'So we'll take you to look at it tomorrow. It's not that far away. Near to where Andy lives, actually.'

I couldn't wait to go and see it.

In the end Prof Charlie and Peter came too. Grandma and Handsome thought they should both be in on it, if we were going to talk Mum and David round.

Grandma had got the keys from the estate agent and we let ourselves in, though we could probably have just pushed down the big front door. The house had been built in 1875, the notes said, and hadn't been lived in for the last two years. It smelled of damp and something decaying in the drains.

'Don't look at it as it is,' advised Handsome. 'Look at its potential.'

At the moment it had the potential to fall down about our ears.

Peter and I looked at each other.

'Let's explore,' we said.

Downstairs was rambling. Corridors seemed to lead here and there for no particular reason. Eventually we found the back door that led out into the garden. We turned the big rusty key in the lock and went outside.

'Wow,' said Peter.

The garden was enormous and very overgrown, but on one side of it we could see an ivy-covered stable block and some outhouses.

'Perfect for Pets' Problems and Handsome's building business,' I muttered.

On the other side of the house was an old conservatory with its door half off. We went back into the house that way and climbed up the worn stairs to the upper floors.

I found a quaint little room tucked in under the eaves. It had a window seat and an old tiled fireplace.

'I like this room,' I said.

Peter grunted and crossed the hall.

A bigger room looked out over the front garden.

'There'd be room for all my computer stuff in here,' he said. 'I could leave it all set up, not have to tidy everything away like I do in our flat.'

There were three more bedrooms and a boxroom, so there was room for Mum and David, Grandma and Handsome and the new baby. Peter and I decided that if Handsome could fix this place up, with our help, then it would do nicely.

The only problem now would be convincing Mum. Sorry, Mum and David. I'd have to get used to David being around permanently. Just as Peter would have to get used to Mum.

# 28

The following Saturday Mum and David came back from their honeymoon. We just gave David time to carrying a giggling Mum over the threshold before we pounced. All of us. Prof Charlie, Peter, Grandma, Handsome and me. We showed them the details of the house and before they even had time to unpack, dragged them round there.

'We have to snap it up quickly,' said Handsome, 'before someone else does.'

'So that's why it's been lying empty for two years,' said Mum.

Marriage hadn't made her any less sharp.

'No one's seen its potential yet,' said Handsome. 'Sure it needs a bit of work, but I can do most of that, with some help from the rest of you. You just have to use your imagination to see what it could be like.'

So I wasn't the only one with imagination. Handsome Harris had some too.

Mum picked off a bit of peeling wallpaper and a shower of loose plaster fell on her head.

'And I thought rewiring Pelham Way was bad,' she muttered.

She looked at David. 'What do you think?'

'I think that old conservatory, once it's fixed up, would make a great studio for me. It's south facing and there's so much light. The big walled garden would be great for the baby. Very safe.'

'But the house is falling down and it'll be chaos till it's all fixed up,' wailed Mum, 'I'm not good with chaos.'

'I can do chaos,' I said.

'Me too,' said Peter.

'My speciality,' grinned Grandma.

Everybody laughed and somehow it was settled. Mum got swept along on the tide of everyone else's enthusiasm. She and David put in an offer for the house which was accepted. We move in in a few weeks' time. I can scarcely believe it.

We hardly see anything of Handsome these days. He spends all his time working on the old house, getting a bit of it habitable for Mum and the new baby. I hope this baby can sleep through hammering and banging because there's going to be a lot of it for a while.

Funnily enough, Mum is calmer than she was. I think being pregnant suits her. She's rounder and rosier and looks wonderful. David looks after her like she was fine porcelain. I think she secretly likes that. David's friend has bought his flat, but in the meantime David still goes there every day to work. We all meet up at dinnertime. It's a madhouse. Velvet's timetable looks rather forlorn pinned up on the wall. But then, she did say it didn't work for her family either.

Three Pelham Way is up for sale. I think I would feel more upset about this if I weren't so excited about the new/old house. We've had loads of people come to view our house. Some of them are so rude. They traipse through complaining about the colour of the wallpaper and saying how small the kitchen is. Then they poke about in cupboards looking at the kind of jam we eat. One of them got stuck up in the attic last week. Grandma thought everyone had gone and pushed up the ladder and closed the trapdoor. We only realized when we heard the banging and shouting that there was someone still up there. I thought for a moment we might have a ghost, but this ghost knew too many rude words. We had to cover Mortimer's ears.

And I've had to break the habits of a lifetime and keep my bedroom tidy all the time. It's not easy. Grandma shows the prospective buyers round and explains that she will be removing all the animals and enclosures from the back garden, to say nothing of the luminous dinosaur footprints. The people mostly look relieved. Well, I suppose if they want to lead ordinary boring lives . . . like mine was before Grandma arrived.

Mum goes off to work every day and lets Grandma get on with it.

I go to school every day and try to concentrate on my work, wishing I was at the new-old house helping Handsome. Inside I have this really excited feeling that I usually only get before my birthday or Christmas. There's just so much happening in my life.

Andy says I'm lucky my life is so interesting and he's really pleased that I'll be moving closer to him.

I am too. I may need some advice from him about how to cope with brothers and sisters. I've never had any of these before, and neither has Velvet.

'Perhaps I can come and help with the animals or the building work,' said Andy.

'Don't worry,' I said. 'You'll be roped in right away.'

Velvet volunteered to help too.

'I'll come and help you paint your bedroom. I'm quite good at that. And Mum says she'll come round with loads of food the day you move in, so your mum doesn't have to worry about feeding everyone.'

Miss Flack is already busy making curtains and cushions for the baby's room – in buttermilk yellow, the same colour as Mum's wedding dress, because we don't know if it's a boy or a girl yet. And Mrs Polanski has offered Mum some lovely old furniture that she no longer needs.

'You'll need a lot more stuff to fill that big house,' she said, 'and it's only collecting dust in mine.'

Major Knotts has given Handsome several tins of paint he had left over from his army-surplus shop and Mr and Mrs Hobbs have promised to help with the garden.

'Mr Hobbs just loves to be out in the garden,' smiled Mrs Hobbs, 'and ours is so small. It'll be a real treat for him.'

Everyone has been so kind. It's good to have friends.

# 29

I still haven't decided what to do about my dad.
I haven't forgotten about him. I just haven't
decided yet. I haven't spoken to Mum about
him again, because it didn't seem right somehow
with her just getting married to David and the
baby coming. So, I decided to have a word
with Grandma. She was out in the garden
feeding the ducks and checking on a macaw
she'd just got in who'd been plucking all his
feathers out.

I stroked the macaw, whose name was Dandy.

'I'm still trying to decide what to do about my
dad, Grandma,' I said. 'Whether to see him or
not.'

Grandma stopped scattering the scraps of food.
The ducks gathered round her ankles and
quacked a reminder.

'And?' said Grandma.

'And I wondered what you thought.'

Grandma emptied out the last of the ducks'

food and came and sat on the step of the Pets' Problems shed beside me.

'I think you have to make up your own mind on this one, Abby,' she said. 'I never cared much for your father, as you know, and his recent behaviour hasn't made me change my mind. Why he couldn't just come to the front door and ask to see you instead of parading up and down in a false beard, I'll never know. But, that's just typical of your dad, I'm afraid.'

'Uhuh.' Mum had already said much the same.

'But,' went on Grandma, 'he is your dad, and perhaps everyone deserves a second chance. It's really up to you.'

I nodded, gave Dandy another stroke, and put him back in his cage.

'I'll think about it some more,' I said.

I did, and decided what to do about it.

The school talent contest was due to be held in a few days' time in the school hall. Grandma and I and the pets would be on the stage, and Mum and David, Handsome, Prof Charlie and Peter would be in the audience.

'We'll come and cheer you on,' they said.

But I had six invitations to give out and I still had one left, so I decided to send it to my dad. I didn't say 'Please come' or 'I'll look forward to seeing you' or anything like that. I just sent the invitation which showed me as one of the competitors, and I waited to see what would happen.

Cosgrove High was buzzing before the talent show. Everyone had their favourite to win the contest. Some people even thought I might.

'Your performance is really different,' said Velvet.

'And funny,' said Andy

'We'll see,' I said. 'I wonder what the teachers will do?'

Everyone had been wondering about that. But the teachers still weren't saying.

On the night of the contest there was to be a teacher's performance between each pupil's performance. Grandma and I were on after Mrs Jackson.

In class we had tried to winkle out of her what she was going to do, but she just smiled and said, 'Wait and see.'

Belinda and the Beelines had been practising every day in school so everyone knew what they were doing. To be fair, and I hate to be fair to them, they did sound good.

Funnily enough, Belinda has backed off a bit since I bopped her. I know it was the wrong thing to do and I'm not proud of it, but now she's only nasty to me when she's surrounded by the Beelines.

Why are some people like that? Why do they have to pick on people? Does it make them feel better, or bigger, or more important? For a while

Belinda and the Beelines gave Velvet a hard time because of the colour of her skin. Then, rumour has it, Mrs Jackson had a word with them, and since then they've left Velvet alone.

When Belinda's alone she gives me a wide berth now. Suits me fine. We're never going to be friends.


I was really nervous on the night of the contest. Nervous and excited.

'That's the best way to be,' said Grandma. 'That way you'll give a good performance.'

Mum gave me a big hug before I left for the school with Grandma and the pets.

'You'll be great,' she said. 'Break a leg.'

'Just an old theatrical saying,' said David, when I looked aghast. 'It means good luck.'

He gave me a hug too. I liked that. He was kind and funny, but he wasn't my dad and didn't try to be. I liked that too.

Handsome drove us to the school in a super-clean Dusty and we gathered with the rest of the competitors backstage. Handsome joined Mum and the others in the hall. Andy and Velvet appeared backstage too, as they had promised. It was madness back there, all noise and confusion till the Drama teacher appeared and quietened everybody down. She lined us all up in order of performance, and threatened us with dire consequences if we chattered once the performances got underway. Grandma got talking to Mrs Jackson. We still didn't know what she was going to do because she was covered from head to toe in a long black cloak.

Then we fell silent as we heard Mr Doig welcome everyone to the Cosgrove High Talent Contest. The audience coughed, settled down and the hall lights dimmed. The talent contest had begun. We could hear what was going on and caught occasional glimpses of the performances through the side curtains. It all seemed to be going very well. I remembered not to chatter, but I was shaking with excitement. I could have fallen over and broken a leg quite easily.

The backstage queue of performers moved up quietly till it was Mrs Jackson's turn. Then, with a dramatic flourish, she threw off her long cloak and stepped out into the spotlight.

Everyone gasped in surprise. Now everyone knew what she was going to do. Now everyone knew she was a secret belly dancer.

'Good for her,' mouthed Grandma, and I knew Mrs Jackson had gone up several points in her estimation.

Mrs Jackson wobbled her belly and rolled her hips in time to the music and got a thunderous round of applause. And a lot of wolf whistles. She'd never live it down, of course, but she now had her place in the history of Cosgrove High. I don't know if she was a good belly dancer or not, but to appear in that costume in Cosgrove High's school hall took real guts, and all the pupils knew that. She went up in their estimation too.

Aren't teachers surprising sometimes?

Then it was our turn. Gulp. Help. It's all a mistake. I want to go home.

But Grandma gave me a wink, and we were on. Fortunately, because of the bright lights on stage I couldn't see the audience too clearly, and I had warned Mum, within an inch of her life, not to call out or wave.

Mortimer started off our routine by doing a little dance on his perch and saying, 'Hello, hello, hello,' to the audience, like we'd taught him. Benson just about wagged his tail off. We didn't need to teach him to do that. He's a limelight case anyway. Then Grandma strummed on her guitar and gave me a key. G, I think it was. Not that I'd know. Not that it mattered, since we both knew I'd never sing in it anyway. I began my performance.

At first there was a kind of embarrassed silence from the audience. People looked at each other and made 'Oh dear, dear' faces. Then, when Benson began to howl and Mortimer shouted at me 'Get off, Get off!' and 'Rubbish, Rubbish!', they realized it was meant to be a joke and fell about.

We sang an extra song as an encore because the audience clapped so much. Grandma and I took lots of bows. I really liked that. I could get used to being a star. There was extra-loud clapping coming from the end of one row. I guess that's where Mum and the others were sitting. But, even though I screwed up my eyes and peered out into the audience, I couldn't see my dad, with or without a black beard.

There were two more performances after ours, then it was all over. Everyone was giggly and chatty. Even the teachers. The judges, who included the Chairman of the Board of Governors (I hoped Mr Doig hadn't told him I was the Alien girl) went into a huddle and muttered to themselves about the winners. It was an agonizing time.

The prize for the 'Most Talented Teacher' was announced first. It was no surprise that it went to Mrs Jackson. She accepted the trophy with a smile and a little wiggle of her gold-belted hips. The audience went wild.

Then the judges spoke a little bit about all the pupil competitors. Grandma and I and the pets were highly commended for our original act and good use of natural ability, i.e. my inability to sing in tune. The judges thought we were very funny and said they hadn't laughed as much in a long time.

But we didn't win.

Belinda and the Beelines won.

The judges said they had obviously worked very

hard at their presentation and deserved to win, though they advised them to take a leaf out of our book and try to be more original and not copy other people's style.

Belinda would be unlivable with now.

But we all clapped when she stepped forward to receive the Cosgrove High Talent Contest trophy.

Then the Drama teacher came on stage with a huge bouquet of flowers. Belinda stepped forward again to receive them. 'Oh thank you. Thank you. You're too kind,' she said, arms outstretched, big smile on her face.

But the Drama teacher walked past her – everybody tittered – and presented them to me. 'These were handed in for you a few moments ago,' she whispered.

'Thank you,' I said, and buried my nose in the delicate lemon roses to cover my confusion. I thought they had something to do with the contest, a prize for being runner-up, or something. It wasn't until I got home and was unwrapping them to put them in water that I found the card.

*You were great. You have the same voice as me.*
*Call me, if you want to.*
*Love, Dad xx*

I put the flowers in a glass vase on the coffee table in the sitting room. Prof Charlie and Peter had come back for supper, and this tiny house, which would soon no longer be ours, was noisy with everyone talking about the contest and how they thought Grandma and I should have won. Naturally.

I slipped upstairs to my bedroom. Rosie was waiting for me, curled up on her pink blanket on my bed. I picked her up and held her to my cheek. With my free hand, I fished out a little card from the drawer in my bedside table. I looked at it for a moment, then I took a deep breath, took out my mobile phone, and called my dad.

## ABBY: CALAMITY AND CHAOS

*Margaret Ryan*

Abby can't wait for the arrival of her wild Grandma Aphrodite from Oz – and when they meet, she's not disappointed!

In her sheepskin coat, crocodile boots and sixties' clothes (not to mention that mysterious trunk – what could be inside it?), Aphrodite walks into Abby and her mum's life and turns it upside down.

Before long, they're dancing to The Beatles, bringing chaos to the neighbourhood, and hatching a brilliant plan to find Mum a man . . .

*By the winner of the Scottish Arts' Council Book Award.*

## ABBY: MADNESS AND MAYHEM

Nothing's been the same since Grandma Aphrodite came to stay from Australia. For starters, Abby's mum has finally found a boyfriend, and is acting like a teenager.

And now Grandma's husband, Handsome Harris, has disappeared. Could he *really* have been kidnapped by the Australian mafia?

One thing's for sure, Abby and her grandma will soon be hot on Handsome's trail . . .

## KAT McCRUMBLE

*Margaret Ryan*

This is the first story about Kat McCrumble and her many pets.

Kat is happy helping her father run the Crumbling Arms. But trouble is brewing – the big hotel is trying to force them out of business, and worse still, badger baiters have been spotted nearby.

What can Kat do? Kat can get mad, that's what, and when that happens the world had better watch out! She hasn't got the McCrumble red hair for nothing . . .

## SIMPLY KAT McCRUMBLE

*Margaret Ryan*

Another Auchtertuie adventure!

Kat's real passion is, of course, animals. She and her dad will look after anything, from donkeys to tarantulas.

Now they've given a home to their most unusual animal yet: a cute little wallaby called Wilf. He's a real character and soon has tourists flocking to see him. Then Wilf is kidnapped and Kat is furious. And when that happens, look out world!

## WILD KAT McCRUMBLE

*Margaret Ryan*

Kat's wild about animals. She and her dad run the Crumbling Arms inn and animal sanctuary, deep in the Scottish Highlands. It's chaotic, but fun.

Then one day a strange McCrumble called Vladimir arrives and claims that the inn is rightfully his. Kat and her dad could lose their home. And, if that isn't bad enough, someone has been trying to poison the local wildlife. This makes Kat really wild, but, as always, she has a plan . . .